THE INCREDIBLE MAGIC OF BEING

by Kathryn Erskine

Scholastic Inc.

ISBN 978-1-338-23853-2

10 9 8 7 6 5 4 3 2   17 18 19 20 21

Printed in the U.S.A.   40

First printing 2017

Book design by Maeve Norton

To the thinkers and dreamers—
keep believing.

—KE

1

BLACK HOLES AND MESSIER OBJECTS

Magic is all around us, but most people never see it.

Sometimes even I can't.

Like right now.

I'm in the backseat holding my breath, leaning away from the black hole and trying not to get sucked in.

The black hole is my sister. She didn't used to be a cosmic phenomenon, but something happens to people when they become teenagers and their brains explode. Pookie's went supernova. When she was twelve she was very high functioning, but now that she's fourteen she makes this noise like an orangutan, wears earbuds and sunglasses even inside, and has a Moody Place behind the house where she goes when she's mad, which is most of the time. I call her Spooky. Only in my head, though. I'm not stupid.

"Mom! Joan!" Pookie yells. "Tell Julian to stop kicking my bag!"

"I wasn't kicking your—"

Mom pumps the brakes. I think she's doing it more to get our attention than for driving purposes. It makes me feel like puking again.

"Julian, honey, try to stop jiggling your feet so much. Calming breaths, remember?"

Joan looks back and gives me a wink that means, *Hang in there, kiddo.*

I try to hold my legs still and take a really deep breath.

"You don't have to suck all the air out of the van, freak," Pookie hisses.

When I turn to answer my foot touches her KEEP OUT bag, which doesn't even have anything good in it. I've checked.

She makes her orangutan noise in my face, so I squish over to my side like a dwarf star resisting the gravitational pull of the black hole, even though my door smells like puke with a twist of lemon-fresh wipe because I threw up on it in Delaware. Or maybe it was New Jersey. Probably both. Plus Connecticut. Motion sickness is a problem I have. It's why I don't like car rides or boats. Especially boats. I've never actually been on a boat, but I want to puke just thinking about it.

Plus, you can drown.

Mom says you have to deal with your fears to overcome them. So I saved up my allowance and bought a life jacket, which I'm already wearing because our new house in Maine is on a lake. I saw it on Google Maps. The lake is way closer to the house than necessary, which means tsunamis. Technically they're only in the ocean, but this lake is big and it's close to the ocean. It could have a mini tsunami . . . a tsunamini.

Pookie says I'm highly abnormal for a nine-year-old and should be put in a lab at Caltech and studied like a mutant rat.

I think with a name like Pookie you should be careful what you say.

My foot touches her bag again and I hope she doesn't notice, but that's like hoping Mom won't notice if I bring a Labrador retriever home.

Pookie points to my telescope on the seat behind us. "Touch my bag one more time and I'm throwing your stupid telescope out the window!"

I hug my knees to my chest, take a deep breath, and remind myself that the magical thing about super massive black holes like Pookie is that they emit quasars, the brightest objects in the entire universe. I keep waiting for that to happen with Pookie, but I think this is one of those situations where I'd have to say, *Don't hold your breath*.

So I let my breath out, which makes her go all orangutan and snarl at me like I'm a worthless Messier Object.

FART!

(FART stands for "Facts and Random Thoughts." Plus, it's fun to say *fart*.)

MESSIER OBJECTS

Messier Objects are not messier like my room,
or Pookie's that's even messier. Mr. Messier was
a French guy who was looking for comets, but
certain objects—the stars and galaxies and
stuff—got in the way, so he made this list of
not comets so he wouldn't get confused.

Did you know that if you find a comet you get to name it after yourself? That's what I'm going to do. Then I can live forever.

No, really. I have a Dobsonian Orion XT8 telescope. It's good enough to see the Dog Star (the best star in the whole universe), all the Messier Objects, *and* comets as long as you're not in the city, where there's too much light to see hardly anything.

That's how come I think it's awesome we're moving to Maine. No light pollution! I'll find a comet pretty fast. Then I'll have lots of time left over to show my family the magic of the universe. Once I figure out how to make them listen.

2

MATT DAMON AND THE BVM

Pookie screeches something in orangutan which I don't catch, but Mom does because she's clairvoyant that way, just like she knows when you've used the gas stove to make s'mores even if she was at work when you did it.

She jerks the Odyssey into a gas station and market, and Pookie sprints to the outdoor restrooms. She stops at the dirty ladies' room door that has no knob and turns back to glare at Mom as if Mom is sacrificing her to medical science.

Mom puts her head down on the steering wheel and breathes like Darth Vader.

Joan reaches over and squeezes her shoulder. Joan is a physical therapist as well as a paramedic, so she's really good at squeezing shoulders.

I look at the men's room door to see if it's any cleaner so Pookie can use that, but it's even worse. That's when I see the gas station sign and read it out loud. "*Sav-U-More Grotto with BVM.* What's a BVM?"

"Blessed Virgin Mary," Joan says.

Mom turns her head to Joan without lifting it from the steering wheel, and her voice cracks like maybe she's about to cry. "What would the Virgin Mary be doing at a gas station?"

"She's probably in the grotto," I point out. "That means a little cave."

"Oh," says Mom, "that explains it," and starts laughing, so I know the shaky voice isn't crying, which is a relief until her laughing sounds kind of crazy.

"Mom? Are you all right?"

Joan starts laughing, too. "She's just de-stressing from the long drive, kiddo. It's OK."

Pookie sits down so hard the whole van bounces and slams the door. "It is so *not* okay!" She rips half a dozen wipes out of the Clorox container, and the lemon smell makes me want to puke again. She opens her mouth and takes a deep breath.

My stomach gets tight and I can tell she's about to go supernova, which might put Mom over the edge. I quickly say, "Matt Damon is trying to get clean toilets for everyone."

She stops scrubbing her hands and stares at me, but not with the mushy eyes she usually has if I pull Matt Damon out of my back pocket. "Well, why isn't he here?"

"I don't know, but the Blessed Virgin Mary is. Do you want to see her?"

"Shut. Up."

"No, really." I crane my neck, and beyond the men's room I see a stone path and a little wooden sign down low that says GROTTO WITH BVM.

"She's down there. I'm going."

"Julian!" all three of them yell at once.

"We have to meet the moving van," Joan says, "and we're late. It's already there."

At least Mom drives past the path so I can look down to the grotto and see the BVM. She has her hand up, waving, so I wave back. It's not much of a meeting.

"I don't see why I couldn't have said a quick hello."

"It's a statue, you freak," Pookie hisses.

Joan turns and glares at her. "Hey! Watch it."

"Mary could be magic," I point out. "She's very religious."

Pookie rolls her eyes. "We're not even Catholic!"

"We can learn much from those who are different," Mom says.

"A statue? Really, Mom?" Pookie turns her music up so loud I can hear it through her earbuds. I want to tell her she's going to go deaf, but we've had this discussion before and she says she doesn't want to hear it, which is pretty funny when you think about it because that's exactly the point. She's not going to hear it if she keeps blasting music at her eardrums because she'll be DEAF!

FART!

LIFE AFTER DEATH

I want to talk to the BVM because I'd like to know if she can give me some input on what happens to you after you die.*

*This is more of a random thought than a fact, but that's covered in FARTS (Facts and Random Thoughts).**

I like to use asterisks because they remind me of stars.*

Joan says when I write a real paper I have to use numbered footnotes because asterisks get confusing. I see her point.*

****But I'm still going to use them!

Carl Sagan, this famous astronomer, said, "We are made of star-stuff." That's because stars have hydrogen and helium at their core, and those elements combine to make other elements, which are what we're made up of. So I think when we die we end up in the stars. I can't ask Carl Sagan because he's already dead, probably in a star, but it makes sense. When we die we have to go SOMEwhere because there's a scientific principle called conservation of matter, which means stuff doesn't disappear, it just changes form. Like when you boil water and eventually the pot is empty because it all boiled away? It didn't really go away. It turned into steam and now it's in the air we breathe. See? The universe is full of magic.

When I die, which I don't want to but I know I will, I'm pretty sure I'm going to end up in Sirius, the Dog Star, because I have a special connection with dogs. They run away from their humans just to kiss me. When their humans say, "Hey! Come back here!"

I tell them, "It's OK, I'm going to die and be in the Dog Star! And your dog knows that so we're bonding!" which calms the humans down because they stand really still and stare at me until their dogs go back to them.

Anyway, I want my family to be able to find me when I'm up in the Dog Star, so they have to get better at looking through a telescope and seeing the Messier Objects before I die. Right now, all they say is, "That's nice, honey" (Mom) or, "Those are some messy objects all right" (Joan) or, "This is so stupid! I can't see anything!" (Pookie). I want to tell her it's easier to see through a lens if you stop rolling your eyes, but if I did she'd go all supernova on us and then Mom would get upset and then Joan would get mad and then the Messier Objects might get blown out of the universe, so I have to be patient. When they learn where the Dog Star is they can talk to me even when I'm dead. It's really important to talk to people after they die so they won't be lonely.

I know that because I'm a uni-sensor. That's what I call sensing information from the universe. It's not like someone's actually telling me something. I just know. Pookie says I have Mutant Brain Syndrome and think too much. But I'm not actually thinking; stuff just comes into my head randomly. I don't ask for it. Mom says I'm uniquely gifted and should cultivate my gift so I can do something amazing with my life. Joan says people should stop labeling me, and let me be a kid.

I like Joan a LOT.

Mom looks up at the rearview mirror, which is how she talks to me when she's driving. "I'm sorry, honey. We'll come back and visit later. Right now, we don't have time."

Grown-ups always say, "We don't have time" or, "There's no time for that," which isn't actually true. Time is infinite. It's a question of how you choose to use it.

3

TIME

Time is really important, but nobody understands it. Not even physicists. They're sitting around watching *The Big Bang Theory* and eating Go-Gurts waiting for someone like Newton or Einstein to have a brilliant moment and explain it to them.

FART!

TIME

There's a physicist named Julian (like me!) Barbour who says there's not just now, but lots of different nows. Which I guess means lots of different thens. And lots of different futures. I think that sounds cool. I'd like to hang out in some other nows, especially if they're not inside this car and not next to Pookie, who just took her earbuds out and is glaring at me. I don't know why. I didn't even fart. That time.

Mostly we think of time like this: "Yesterday I left my house in Washington, DC, and today I'll get to my new house in Maine." That's the way Newton saw it, but then Einstein came along and said space and time are related. So, if I'd taken a spaceship from DC to Maine by way of another galaxy at almost the speed of light, then even if we all arrived at the same second, everyone else would've aged more in those two days than me. Isn't that cool? It's because by going through space so fast you kind of beat time.

Actually, you bend it. Which I don't quite understand, but that's OK because even physicists get confused by this stuff.

It's too bad Mom couldn't have used the warp speed method, because she looks five years older than yesterday. When I point that out, Pookie snorts and puts her earbuds back in but one side of her mouth curls up, which makes me happy because usually she doesn't listen to anything I say anymore, and if she does she tells me I'm stupid.

Mom does not smile, however. She's so cranky she won't even let me explain Einstein's theory. I don't like it when people won't listen. "How about the block theory of time, then? It's different from Einstein's theory because it says the past, present, and future are all blocks and—"

"Julian!" Mom says all shout-y, but Joan looks over at her and says, "Michelle" in her calm voice so Mom takes a deep breath. "Not now. Another time, OK?"

But that's just it. This might be the only now we have together. There may not be another one.

4

ORION

"Your mother will never go for this," Joan says.

We're standing in a super awesome tree house next to our new real house.

"But it's the perfect bedroom for me! I'm closer to the stars this way. It's like being in my own planetarium."

She gives me a *Yeah, right* look.

"I bet you could convince her. Look, I'm right next door. If you leave a window open I could yell and she could hear me."

Joan looks at the house, back to where we're standing, and back to the house again like she's measuring the distance.

Joan is the newest addition to our family, but she understands me the best. She's not all helicopter-y like Mom. In fact, when Mom gets too panicky, Joan does this great whoop-whoop-whoop-whoop-whoop helicopter sound and even though Mom glares at her, at least she backs off a little.

"OK, kiddo, I'll see what I can do."

"Yes! I love Maine!" I yell at the exact same time Pookie yells from inside, "I hate Maine!"

Joan sighs. "I better go help your mother."

Which is disappointing because I really wanted Joan to look through my telescope so I could show her the general vicinity of Sirius, the Dog Star. She's the one most likely to actually listen to me and understand how important it is to see the magic in the universe. Plus, she helped me set up my telescope. It's heavy and fragile because we got it off Craigslist and the mirror is a little loose. Joan has a lot of experience hauling heavy, fragile objects, which are injured people since she's a paramedic. We set it up on a little patio in the middle of the yard where there's a fire pit, but Mom says we're not using that because fires are dangerous so it's perfect for my telescope.

FART!

ORION AND SIRIUS

Orion is not just the name of my telescope. It's also that cool constellation of the Hunter that's easy to find because it looks sort of like an H. Orion has three Messier Object numbers: M_{42}, M_{43}, and M_{78}. (There are 110 Messier Objects and they all start with M, which you can probably figure out why.) Orion's sword, which is below his belt, contains the Orion Nebula (M_{42}), which is where stars are born. No, really. And now I can watch the magic happen.

Also, Orion's belt points to Sirius, the Dog Star, which is in the constellation Canis Major (M₄₂). If you count about eight belt lengths down to the left, there's Sirius! It's so easy even my family can learn, eventually.

I want to keep looking at the universe, but I have to run inside because Pookie is heading supernova. Our new house has something called "Jack and Jill" bedrooms that are connected by a bathroom. She says it's a violation of the Constitution's Eighth Amendment (cruel and unusual punishment) for a fourteen-year-old girl to share a bathroom with her nine-year-old brother.

"There's no other option," Mom says, holding her head and leaning against the kitchen counter. "We have a master bedroom and the Jack and Jills."

"And four more bedrooms!" Pookie says.

"That brand-new addition is for the bed-and-breakfast. We're renting them out."

"You're not renting them out tonight!"

"Those are your rooms, and you need to get used to it," Mom says.

Joan opens her mouth to speak, but I beat her to it.

"I can use the bathroom downstairs and sleep in the tree house!"

"There is no way you're sleeping in a tree house," Mom says. "It's totally unprotected."

Occasionally Mom responds well to humor, so I grin, clutch my life jacket, and say, "See? I've got protection!"

She shakes her head.

"There are no actual humans around, Mom," Pookie says, "in case you hadn't noticed."

"There are mosquitoes, which carry disease," Mom says.

"Ah," says Joan, "I thought of that."

We all stare at her. She never thinks of stuff like that. You'd think she would because she's a paramedic, but Mom is the one who worries about everything.

Joan pulls a lacy curtain thing out of a duffel bag. "It's a mosquito net. Now he can be safe in the tree house."

The rest of us are still staring at her.

She shrugs. "The guys at the station gave it to me as a joke at my farewell party."

"Problem solved!" says Pookie.

Mom is not convinced. "What if the boards are rotted?"

"I stomped on them," Joan says.

"What if he rolls over in his sleep and falls out?"

Joan sighs. "The railing is secure. I tested it."

"What if there's an emergency?"

"He can take your cell phone for the night."

Mom closes her eyes. "Just this once."

Joan winks at me. *Just this once* is Mom's way of saying, *We'll try it because I'm too tired to fight but I'm scared and I don't expect it to work.* But sometimes it does and then she's OK with it.

That's what's going to happen with my tree room.

Mom insists on watching me climb up the ladder to my tree room because she thinks I might fall. Joan stands behind her and gives me a nod and thumbs-up, which means just do what Mom says because it's easier that way.

As soon as Mom goes inside I climb back down because I want to look through my telescope some more. The universe is amazingly clear and bright with no light pollution! You almost feel like you can touch the stars. It's magic.

It makes me feel like the night a couple of years ago when the whole neighborhood watched the International Space Station pass across the sky. We stood outside for the entire time, which was only about four minutes, but still, we watched it move like a really bright star arcing across the vast darkness. We were all in awe, thinking, *There are real people up in that tiny starlike thing*, and we all felt connected for a few minutes and even waved and said, "Hey, guys," or maybe the talking part was just me. At any rate, it was a very special moment for everyone, and that feeling of being together was so strong I'll never forget it. I want to have that for all eternity, especially after I'm dead.

When I'm so tired my eyes won't focus no matter how I turn the eyepiece, I go to my new tree room and lie down on my yoga mat and look up at the sky. It's like living in my own planetarium. With a mosquito net over it.

I smile and take a deep breath. It smells like Christmas. That's because there are so many pine trees around. Plus, it feels like Christmas because this place is magic.

The only bad thing is hearing the water of the lake lapping against the shore. I hope I don't have any drowning nightmares. Then I'm mad that I thought about drowning nightmares because a lot of times when I think of something it comes true, even if I don't want it to. I check that my life jacket is secure and force my eyes open to look at the stars so they're the last thing on my mind and I can dream of finding my comet.

Maybe tomorrow night. I have to find it before the other comet searchers out there. Sometimes, when it's really important to you, you can do magical things.

5

THE COSMOS

A hard plastic mask is on my face and people tell me to breathe but the air is outside the mask not inside and I try to push it off but they hold me down and press the mask over my nose and mouth and then the world gets blurry and sounds bubbly and far away just like it always does when this happens but you can't stop it and then everything goes black and you drown.

Do you ever have that nightmare? Me too. It happens a lot. This time I wake up with the mosquito net on my face and I hear the water in the lake and even though I'm realizing I haven't actually drowned I still gulp in big breaths of air. I feel pretty freaked but I'm not telling Mom or she'll say, *See, I told you the tree house was a bad idea.*

I might tell Joan because she'll say, *Sounds scary, kiddo, but you're OK,* and then squeeze my shoulder so it seems like it was OK to be scared of drowning but it's not such a big deal because actually it was just a dream. Then we'll talk about the cosmos, which is another way of saying the universe, because she knows that always calms me down. I mean, how can you be upset when you're talking about something as magical as that?

It's like what Joan says about peanut butter chocolate chip macadamia nut cookies: "What's not to love?"

I love the cosmos, which is why I've studied it my whole life and know a lot about it. I also love dogs (especially Labrador retrievers), Italian, Harry Potter, passion fruit juice, yoga (only one kind, though), marshmallows, this TV show called *MacGyver*, rocks, global sanitary issues, and a bunch of other stuff, but they're all part of the universe so I figure they're covered.

FART!

THE COSMOS =
THE ORDER OF THE UNIVERSE, SORT OF

Cosmos means the order of the universe, except the universe isn't really orderly. It's more like when kids are lined up for recess and it's sort of a line but arms and legs are sticking out and someone's hopping in place and someone's shoving off the wall, and someone needs the restroom and a fight might break out but basically you know that the kids will make it out to the playground and fan out in a scatter formation but stay on the playground, mostly. A siren might go off and some kids will scream and run in circles, and there's always the possibility of a UPS truck losing its brakes and skidding onto the playground, scattering everyone, or a meteor hitting right next to the swings, you never know, but basically that's what orderly chaos looks like. And then you go back inside for language arts.

My family is like orderly chaos, too. There was a lot of shouting and running around in our new house last night, and also this morning, but basically I know that the coffeepot will be on, there'll be something for breakfast, more boxes will be unpacked, and there might even be photos of us up on the wall. And Pookie will be in a bad mood, which Mom will try to deflect. *Deflect* means to change the subject and hope the person you're talking to won't notice. It doesn't work with Pookie, but Mom keeps trying.

I just hope Mom doesn't call a family meeting. Family meetings should be about cool stuff like we're going to a planetarium or we're going to Italy or even we're having marshmallows for dinner every night this week, but they never are. Lately, the best you can hope for in our family meetings is that they're boring. At least the boring ones don't give me an upset stomach.

"Julian!" Mom calls from the bottom of the tree. "I'm here to watch you come down safely, and then we're having a family meeting."

"Asciugamano!" I mutter. Why did I let my brain think about a family meeting?

*It's OK. Uh-shoog-uh-MAHN-oh is not a swear word. It's actually Italian for *towel*. But it sounds like a swear word because it's got the *sh* sound and it feels really good in your mouth.

6

DARK MATTER, DARK ENERGY, AND THE ELEPHANT IN THE ROOM

Mom has the kitchen looking like a normal kitchen, practically. She must've gotten up really early, because the coffee smells at least two hours old, all burned and sour. I don't know how people can drink that stuff.

Our new house is Victorian, which means old and frilly, but the kitchen is modern. There's a sink with a tall curved spigot like you'd see in a lab. I didn't notice it last night. I walk over to it immediately, and just as immediately Mom knows what I'm thinking.

"No experiments, Julian. It might look like a science lab, but it's a kitchen."

"Well," Joan says, "experiments are OK as long as they're supervised."

"By me." Mom glares at us with her hands on her hips.

Joan and I look at each other like Mom is the principal, and not a happy one.

Mom is still having a hard time getting over the Diet Coke and Mentos fountain I made for her birthday. It was magical and also spectacular. I guess it would've been more magical if I'd done it outside instead of in the basement.

Mom wanted to know what on earth I was thinking.

I was thinking that it was February and Mom hates the cold so I didn't want to make her stand outside. Plus, it was last year so my brain wasn't as developed. I still think a Diet Coke and Mentos fountain is magical. And anyway, *Diet* Coke doesn't have sugar so the ceiling and floor and walls weren't that sticky.

I think she was grumpier than usual because it was February, which Mom calls the longest month even though it's the shortest. She says she goes stir-crazy. Magically for us, the Dog Star is brightest in winter when she'll need it the most. The Dog Star may be the only way Mom makes it through February. Especially in Maine, because she says the winters are brutal.

"Sit down, everyone," Mom says and gives a long sigh.

I quickly speak before Mom can start the meeting. "Everyone is invited to look through my telescope tonight. I'm going to teach you how to find Sirius, the Dog Star. It's where—"

"Honey, we'll get to that later," Mom says. "Right now, I really need to tell you the projects you have to work on today so our bed-and-breakfast will be ready for business."

It's my turn to give a long sigh.

That's when I hear the orangutan groan and realize the pile of blankets on the bench is actually Pookie.

Mom pats her back. "Come on, honey, this'll be fun." She's

using her perky voice, which always makes me smile. I bet it's what she sounded like when she was a little girl.

"Stop grinning, freak," Pookie says, squinting at me. "Can't you tell she's about to make us work?"

"This is a family project," Mom says.

"I didn't get a vote," Pookie says.

"You're fourteen. We know what's best for the family."

"Oh, so pulling me out of school and moving me to this deadwater just because you didn't want to be a doctor anymore and you have to homeschool Julian because he's a freak—"

"Pookie!" Mom and Joan shout.

Mom and Pookie yell at each other while I hold my stomach because it feels like my intestines are getting all tangled up. The meeting gets better fast when Joan yells at everyone to sit down and shut up. Everyone does because Joan has authority. She was in the Marines. The Merchant kind, which I don't know what it is, but that's where she learned to swear, according to Mom.

Joan says there are two goals, whether we like them or not, and now we can get to work:

1. Get the house ready for B&B guests (B&B means bed-and-breakfast, which is like a little hotel, but you get extra treats like eating morning glory muffins for breakfast with the family that owns the B&B, which I'm not sure is actually a treat since our family includes Pookie)

2. Be a good and happy host, or at least act like it in front of the guests

Mom and Joan leave a list of chores for each of us, so Pookie's arguing was pointless. Mom heads to the van to get the license for the B&B, and Joan goes to her Outback to get her license for being a paramedic in Maine.

Pookie yells after them, "Did either of you ask my father?"

Mom and Joan lose their smiles and look at each other with eyes that say, *Help!*

My stomach is so tight it feels like my intestines just made a pretzel knot.

FART!

(This is a really big one but it's important.)

DARK MATTER, DARK ENERGY, AND THAT ELEPHANT

Earth and everything on it (including us) and all the other planets are full of atoms. They're the little tiny particles you can't see that we're all made of. They're always moving even though we can't feel it. Just like Earth is always spinning around and orbiting the sun at the same time but we never get dizzy from it. Plus, meteors are flying past and barely missing Earth (in astronomical terms, at least) and stars are exploding and isn't it weird how there's all this craziness happening in our universe but we don't feel it? It's scary to think about all the craziness out there. It kind of makes Mom forgetting the chocolate syrup and having to drink regular milk not such a big thing. Unless you're Pookie. Then the universe is going to explode.

Anyway, we and all the other things that are made of atoms make up less than 5 percent of the universe. Which makes sense if you look at a picture of the solar system and see all that empty space around the sun and planets. And it's dark. So dark matter is this stuff, which we don't know what it is (even physicists because they don't know everything). What we do know is that it tries to hold things together. It's part of what helped make planets to begin with, we just don't know how. Pretty cool, huh? Dark matter makes up less than one-quarter of the universe.

You're probably thinking, "If everything we see makes up less than 5 percent of the universe, and dark matter makes up less than 25 percent, that's not even one-third, so what's the rest of the stuff that's out there?"

Good question.

It's called dark energy and it's like taking every superhero's worst enemy and making a super-galactic Team of Evil out of them.

It's a powerful force that's trying to rip the universe apart.

I know.

Scary.

But don't worry, because it's not going to happen anytime soon. I don't think. Although the universe is expanding faster than physicists originally thought, so now it may be only millions of years instead of kajillions.

In our family the dark matter, the stuff that holds things together, is Mom and Joan. And like a real physicist, I don't really understand them. For one thing, they're grown-ups; for another, they're my parents.

And even though I said before that Pookie is a black hole, I think she's really more like dark energy because she's always trying to rip us apart. I know she's only one person and she's not very big, but she takes up over two-thirds of the room when she talks, and two-thirds of the energy, and two-thirds of the ickiness.

And what gives dark energy its power is an elephant.

Do you know what it means when people say *the elephant in the room*?

I didn't, either, but I asked and what it means is this:

There's not really an elephant in the room. There's some topic that's big and awkward and everyone's ignoring it even though it's really obvious—like if an elephant were standing in the middle of the room and everyone acted like it wasn't there.

In our house, the elephant is Pookie's dad.

She wants to know who he is and where he is and what he's like. And she wants to go live with him.

I don't know why. Mom and Joan aren't perfect, but compared to a lot of moms in books and movies, they're just as good and sometimes a lot better because they're not (1) lying in bed depressed or (2) all upset because they're going through a divorce or (3) dead.

Plus, it's not like her dad has been very dad-like since she was born. She's never seen him. Maybe he doesn't even know how to be dad-like. I think she's taking a big risk.

On the other hand, if she really wants to go find him and live with him, it'd make things a lot easier around here. You'd think Mom and Joan would jump at the chance. They're always saying things like, *I've had just about enough of this!* or, *If you think it's so bad here, you should see how other people live!* etc.

(*Etc.* means there's more examples but either I can't think of them right now or they're all pretty much the same so it gets boring.)

But here's the thing, Mom and Joan are actually upset that Pookie wants to leave. They look like the universe is going to end and they're always whispering and sometimes Mom is crying. See? Dark matter that you don't really understand, all you know is they're trying to hold things together.

Pookie is the dark energy.

And so far, she's winning.

7

PARALLEL UNIVERSES

Mom and Joan drive off without answering Pookie's question about her dad.

"Maybe your dad is in a parallel universe," I tell her.

Pookie tries to deflect. "Have you seen my swim goggles?"

"Maybe they're in a parallel universe, too."

She rolls her eyes. "Is everything better in a parallel universe, dork?"

"Not necessarily. It could be worse. It's just different."

"I have an idea. Why don't you go to a parallel universe? Like now."

"I might be in one already. But then I might break off from that one and go to another, or maybe clone myself and go to multiple universes at once. Isn't that magic?"

Pookie makes her orangutan noise and stomps down the front stairs with her beach towel.

"Do you want to work on our chores together?" I call after her. She always used to make a fun game out of chores.

"I'm not doing any of THEIR chores. This B&B is our parents' stupid idea, not mine." She stalks off to the dock.

The dragon in my stomach starts breathing fire and twisting itself in knots again. If Mom and Joan come home and Pookie hasn't done the jobs on her list, there will be a rift in the space-time continuum.*

*That's not an actual cosmic event, by the way, but it sounds really cool.

I pick Pookie's list up from the floor where she threw it. The first thing she's supposed to do is clean up her room, Jill. I can't do that because if I went in her room I'd be toast, but she's also supposed to get her piles of stuff out of the hall and into Jill, which I do by hurling them through the door without actually stepping inside. Her room is a mess, anyway, except her bed is made because she says that makes a room look neat, and her bedside table has the **DAD Father Daddy** picture frame on it she bought at Target. There's no photo of her dad, though, because we don't have a picture of him.

The next item on her list is to unpack the other boxes of mugs and find a way to get them all in the cupboard. We have a LOT of mugs and right now it's only Mom's favorites that have made it out of the boxes: the really large mugs. I make mug pyramids, which turn out awesome and a little bit like that block-stacking game, Jenga.

Pookie is also supposed to get the downstairs bathroom ready for guests. It looks ready to me, but maybe it needs extra supplies so guests won't run out. I stuff ALL the towels on the bathroom rod in layers because that way you can just take the dirty one off the top and there'll be a clean one underneath. I don't know why nobody thought of that before. I also stack the rolls of toilet paper like columns on either side of the toilet, which looks pretty magical. Now our guests can feel like they're pooping in the Parthenon.

I decide to check my list and do some of my own chores or I'M going to be the one causing the cosmic anomaly. I only have three: "Unpack your room" (that's Jack, not my tree room), "Find presentable clothes for being a host" (I guess Mom wants me to wear shorts that aren't so old; my life jacket is brand-new), and "Set up your bike."

Mom says physical exercise is healthy and important but it's risky and dangerous. So, I have a bike but it's stationary. She's too worried I'll fall and injure myself to let me out on the open road. Or even the open driveway. But I have complete freedom to bike in place as long as I wear a helmet.

Joan already put my bike in its frame, so all I have to do is connect the wires to the battery, which is how I power my flashlight. That's where my pedaling energy goes—to power a light, which is pretty magical when you think about it. If the power of your legs can create light, just think what the power of your mind can do.

Once I'm done with my bike, I go inside to Jack the room to unpack, which means push most of my stuff in the closet. I empty the other boxes onto my floor because that's how my room normally looks.

My bookcase seems sad sitting empty, though, so I unpack my book boxes and line all the books up by size, unless they're a series or a subject and then they have to go together, but I organize them by size within their own subset.

Pookie used to read to me whenever I had a nightmare or couldn't sleep, which means she has read me almost every one of these books at least once. She always knew when I was having a nightmare, or even when I couldn't sleep. She just knew. It was like magic.

Now she doesn't know anymore.

She does—did—great voices. She used to dress us up as book characters for dinner every night, and Mom and Joan had to guess who we were. It was very educational for them. They guessed Jane and Michael Banks from *Mary Poppins* when we sang the nanny song, and *Charlie and the Chocolate Factory* because of the golden ticket, and *The Hobbit* because Pookie made big hairy feet for us, but they didn't get Meg and Mo from *Inkheart* because they'd never read it. After that, I heard Joan reading it aloud to Mom every night, so dressing up for dinner is a good way to get people to read.

Back when Pookie read to me, we were like magnets, stuck together. Now she's turned herself around and we're polar opposites, repelling each other. Joan said maybe Pookie would get nicer in Maine because she wouldn't have any friends and she'd appreciate me again. So far, that hasn't happened. I guess I'll have to go back to having friends in parallel universes. Like Arun.

Arun was my friend in Mumbai who got in a taxi there at the same exact moment I got in one in DC and we both had the identical problem—no seat belt! Mine was broken and he didn't have one at all. We were both really worried that we'd crash and die because our taxi drivers were not exactly responsible, more like insane. Anyway, we talked each other through the whole nightmare, but inside our heads, which is what you do with a friend in a parallel universe; otherwise, people in your own universe get nervous.

I bet Arun and I are going to meet one day, even if it's just passing in an airport and stopping and staring at each other for a moment like we recognize each other from somewhere but we don't remember where, and smiling and nodding and then getting on our separate planes and once we get in our seats realizing that we were the ones who talked to each other as kids and we'll be staring into space with wondrous smiles on our faces and the flight attendant will have to tell us to buckle our seat belts because we're about to take off and we'll laugh because that's exactly what we were scared of when we were boys and then the person in the next seat will stare at us like we're weird but we'll just smile at them because we know we're not weird, we just experienced the magic.

FART!

PARALLEL UNIVERSES

I don't completely understand parallel universes yet because my brain hasn't fully developed and Pookie says it takes MUCH longer for boys' brains to mature so I'll probably be dead before I'm super-smart, but here's what I know now:

I already said that everything in the universe is made up of atoms that are constantly moving. Well, there are particles even smaller than atoms. They have funny names, like if you named all the marshmallows in Lucky Charms cereal, but basically I'll call them quarks (that's a real name). All you have to do is look at something, or someone, and the quarks will change, like turn into a gas from a solid. That's how you can vaporize your sister. (Just kidding.) Some scientists think that quarks actually make copies of themselves so they can be solids and liquids and gasses at the exact same time but not the exact same place so you end up with parallel universes!

I know what you're thinking because I thought it, too. How come we don't see all these parallel universes? Maybe we do! Do you ever wake up from a dream and wonder if the dream was real and what you're waking up to is really the dream? Me too. Maybe that's a parallel universe. And have you ever had anyone say you look just like someone else? It happens to my mom all the time. She says it's because she has red hair and not many people do so she reminds them of another redhead they know. I think it's because she's in parallel universes. I hope so, because she's a good mom and she should spread herself around. I hope

She likes our family best, though. I try not to think about her other families or I get a little jealous. And if I get jealous I might get snarky like Pookie. And if I get snarky Mom might look at me funny and then I'll end up in a parallel universe which might not be as nice as this one. So I usually keep my thoughts to myself. Also because people think I'm weird, which I'm not, I just think about stuff a lot.

I finish putting my books away quickly because thinking about Pookie kind of makes me sad. My Harry Potter books are lined up on top of my bookcase with my wand. They're the most special. I'd like to go to Hogwarts in a parallel universe. And I wish my wand really worked.

I remember I have to find presentable clothes so I drag one of the boxes back out of my closet. It says JULIAN'S LEGACY—CLOTHING. It's my baby stuff and OshKosh B'gosh overalls Mom couldn't give away because they are "adorable," and also my blazer and gray wool pants I wore to the funeral of Joan's coworker who I didn't know but Joan did so Mom said we should all go. The blazer and pants made me feel like I was wearing a uniform at Hogwarts.

I try the pants on and they're OK around the waist but they're about three inches too short and I don't even need Pookie to tell me that they look stupid.

Then I remember researching British schools the first time I read Harry Potter. Do you know that a lot of them, not just

Hogwarts, have uniforms? And when you're in the junior school, which is me, because it's for kids up to age eleven, they wear "short pants"? That's British for "shorts."

By the time Mom and Joan get home, I have a presentable outfit. They get out of their cars all grinning and happy, waving their licenses. They stop smiling when they see Pookie lying on the dock.

Then Mom stares at my presentable pants.

"They were way too short," I explain, "so I made short pants out of them."

Joan loves my presentable pants because she's all about being creative. You can pretty much ruin anything and as long as you're being creative—Joan calls it "using your noggin"—she's OK with it. Once Mom gets over the shock of not getting to keep my funeral outfit as JULIAN'S LEGACY—CLOTHING she decides she likes them, too.

Mom looks back at the dock again. "Please go get your sister," she says, her voice low and quiet, not in a good way. I don't really want to get that close to the water, but I can tell this isn't a good time for a discussion.

I stand on the shore and watch Pookie asleep on the dock. She looks really sweet when she's asleep, even the drooling part. Especially the drooling part. As I watch her, she starts talking really softly. I hate to interrupt conversations, but I don't want Mom to go orbital.

"Hey, Pookie?"

She stops quickly and wipes her mouth but doesn't take off her sunglasses.

I think she's embarrassed so I say, "It's OK to talk to an imaginary friend. It can calm your fears and make you—"

"I'm singing, stupid!"

"Oh. I couldn't tell."

She sits up, whips her sunglasses off, and opens her mouth to yell, but when she actually looks at me she stops. "Why are you dressed like that?"

"I'm a host."

"Yeah, for a mutant parasite. Jeez! Why can't you wear normal shorts?"

"These aren't regular shorts. They're short pants. They're British."

She stands up, grabs her towel, and practically runs to the house. "Mom! Joan! Why are you letting him wear British pants? The stupid life jacket isn't enough?"

By the time I get to the kitchen, Mom and Pookie are already at it and Joan is rubbing her head like she has one of her headaches, which she probably does.

"You, young lady," Mom is yelling, "were supposed to be doing the chores on your list! Instead, your brother is working while you're lounging by the lake!"

"I don't mind," I say quickly. I really hate arguments.

Which is why I'm glad when I hear a voice say, "Excuse me, but what is the meaning of this?"

We all turn to the screen door, where a tall blond man in a tan suit is standing.

Nobody answers so I tell him, "It doesn't actually have any meaning. It's just arguing."

"I'm talking about *that*," the man says, pointing to the left of our house.

"Who are you?" Joan says. "And what are you doing on my porch?" She can be blunt sometimes. A lot.

"I'm Mr. Hale. My client is your next-door neighbor. Who said you could build an addition on this house?"

Joan puts her hands on her hips. "Who said we couldn't?"

"The state of Maine," he says.

"I'm sorry," Mom says, walking over to the screen door and opening it. "I don't understand."

Mr. Hale lets out a big breath and steps inside, just barely. "Look, I'm sorry, too, but that addition is a violation of my client's easement."

"Easement?" Mom says. She sounds like she still doesn't understand.

"Yes, his easement to an unobstructed view of the water, and where you've put your addition completely blocks his view."

"The seller said no one even lived there," Mom says.

"Well, my client does. Only part of the time because he spends most of the year in Florida now that Julia—his wife—has died."

Mom takes in a sharp breath, and I see her eyes dart to me and then look away quickly. I know what she's thinking. *Julia*, like *Julian*. And she's dead. It's what I'm thinking, too.

"If he spends most of the year in Florida," Pookie says, "why does he care?"

"His wife loved that view."

"His wife is dead!" Pookie says.

Mom glares at her. "Pookie!"

I clutch my life jacket. "Did she have a lot of operations?"

"Uh . . . not a lot," Mr. Hale says.

"Was it a heart attack?" I ask.

I hear Mom suck in her breath.

Mr. Hale looks at me like I'm trying to deflect, which I'm not. "No," he says, "cancer. Anyway, the big problem is the easement violation."

Mom and I look at each other, because we know that's not the big problem. A big problem is having multiple medical procedures before you're seven. And a few more after that.

Finally she swallows. "What are we supposed to do?"

"Take down the addition."

"What!" Joan says, plus a lot of swear words, too.

"I hate to be the bearer of bad news," Mr. Hale says, "but even though he's not around much, there's the matter of resale value. Obviously, the property is worth a lot more with a water view."

"Is he selling?" Mom asks.

"We can't afford it," Joan says.

"I don't think it'll be sold until he dies or moves into assisted living because this house is what connects him to Julia. He loved her very much. He's a tough old character, but after losing his wife I think he's dying of a broken heart."

Mom makes a little moaning sound.

I twist my safety bracelet which Mom and I made together. I don't really like it but I have to wear it or she panics. She was so proud that she found a miniature Saturn to put on it. Like a lot of people, she thinks Saturn is every kid's favorite celestial object. Mine is Sirius, obviously, since that's where I'll end up once I'm dead, but I don't think they make charms of the Dog Star.

Pookie glares at me because she says it's annoying when I play with my bracelet. I already stopped biting my nails for Mom and cracking my knuckles for Joan; I can't stop everything. I mean, somebody just died. And her name was Julia.

Scary.

Mom looks at me again and I try hard to give her a calming smile. What Mom—and our neighbor—have to learn is that when Julia, or anyone that sounds like *Julia*, dies the rest of the people have to go on living. They just have to. Otherwise, the person who dies is going to feel terrible! That's too much responsibility to put on a person. They already had to die. They don't need to feel guilty about it!

I'm spinning my bracelet around and around.

Joan says something and then Mom but I don't hear the words. I'm thinking about our neighbor's heart and how it's broken and how he's so sad about Julia he doesn't even want to live. It gives me such a heavy feeling in my chest that it's hard to breathe. When I do take a breath, a moaning sound comes up my throat from deep inside and it hurts a little bit. I think it's my heart crying.

WHEN GALAXIES COLLIDE

It's quiet for a couple of minutes after the lawyer leaves, but my heart is beating loud enough to hear it in my ears, which is not good for it. Pookie pulls my hand away from my safety bracelet so I start saying, *You have to live* in my head. I'm not sure if I'm saying it to our neighbor or to me.

Sometimes, a lot, I say the same thing to myself over and over to calm down. *You have to live, You have to live, You have to live.* I count the syllables on one hand, starting with my thumb, which means I have to say the sentence at least five times so I can always finish on my pinkie. Unless it's a five-syllable phrase, in which case I only have to say it once. But I usually say it more because it doesn't calm you down much if you only say something once. It's better if you say it ten or twenty or one hundred times. It's like what math teachers say about the multiplication table: *Repetition helps.*

Even though I'm talking in my head and counting I still notice Mom and Joan staring at each other and I can feel their shock and confusion. And fear.

"That's that, then," Pookie says. "Let's pack up and go home."

I stop counting my *You have to live* syllables. "But we sold our house. We can't go back there now."

"We'll get another house, stupid. Duh!"

"He's not stupid," Mom says quietly. "He's right. We can't go back. We can't afford another house in DC."

Pookie stares at her. "What are you saying?"

"All our money is tied up in this B&B," Joan says.

"Then we'll sell it and move back."

Joan sits down with a sigh.

Mom clears her throat. "Who's going to buy it now? A B&B that can't be a B&B because the bedrooms have to be torn down?"

Pookie lets out an orangutan scream. "Are you saying we're stuck here? Great! You're supposed to be the adults! You know what's best! What happens now, huh?"

Mom opens her mouth, but her eyes are searching the walls for words.

Pookie answers for her. "Maybe the old guy will croak and then we won't have to worry about it."

"That is not a solution," Mom says.

"Then what's yours," Pookie asks, "since apparently you guys never thought of a plan B?"

Mom turns to look at Joan.

"It'll be fine," Joan says.

Uh-oh. That's what Joan always says when things aren't fine at all and she's figuring out how to start damage control.

Pookie paces back and forth in the kitchen until Mom says, "Kids, why don't you go outside for a bit. Joan and I need to discuss this."

Pookie grabs me by my life jacket and marches me down the front porch stairs and away from the house.

She starts pacing in the front yard. It's giving me motion sickness. I see why Mom sent us outside.

Suddenly, Pookie stops. "You have to go over and talk to the old guy."

"What? Why?"

"Because you look pathetic."

"I'm not pathetic."

"You're wearing a life jacket and British pants. Trust me, you look pathetic."

"What am I supposed to say?"

"That if he makes us tear down the addition, we'll be homeless."

"That's not true. We'll still have the rest of the house."

"We won't have an income, stupid! Money from guests was going to pay the bills. Now there won't be any guests."

I swallow hard and roll my life jacket straps up and try to think. "Joan will still be a paramedic."

"You think that's going to support us? I'd actually like food and clothes, not to mention college. Now go."

"Shouldn't we ask Mom and Joan first?"

"Mom is going to go off the deep end if she doesn't get to do this. She gave up everything and wanted to be this B&B

hostess, and have the chance to homeschool YOU because, let's face it, you're a social anomaly and you'd never make it in middle school."

"I could make it," I say, although I know she's probably right.

"And Joan will freak if Mom freaks. Joan is probably in a panic already."

"Joan? Joan doesn't panic."

"She said, *It'll be fine.* You know what that means. We're toast."

I stare at the house next door.

"Jeez, Julian, I thought you were always trying to make everyone happy."

"I am!"

"Then go!" She turns me around and pushes me next door.

Slowly, I walk over, clutching my life jacket. To be honest, I don't want to talk to him about the addition; I'd rather talk to him about not giving up just because someone you love dies. To be completely honest, I'd rather not have to talk to him at all.

Plus, it feels weird to visit someone when I don't even know his name. I look left to the street and see his mailbox. It says X. SCIACCHITANO on it. Our music teacher in second grade had a first name that started with *Y* and a last name that was long so we called him Mr. Y. I decide to call our neighbor Mr. X. At least he has a name now.

I look at Mr. X's front door and then go to the patio around the back because there are big glass doors and I can see in and he can see out so maybe he'll notice this kid outside and open the door and come out and chat. Maybe. Or not. But I'd rather see him first than go bang on his front door. It's like trick-or-treating. I always hold my breath to see who or what will open the front door. I like front doors with side windows, which his house doesn't have, so you can see the person or monster approaching.

I look inside the patio doors, and when my eyes get adjusted to the darkness I see something special. A BVM! Even though it's a sketch I still recognize the Blessed Virgin Mary, probably because of the halo. She's smiling at me. I smile back and wave. I think it's a good sign.

All over the wall are more drawings, mostly of dogs. I love dogs! I've always wanted a dog! When I stare closer I realize they're all the same dog, just at different ages. It's a black Lab, my favorite! That must be a good sign, too. There are also some sketches of a lady at different ages, maybe Mrs. X. And there are a few photos of boats, which I try to ignore because they make me feel queasy.

I see a big glossy photo on the coffee table of Mr. and Mrs. X. At least, I think that's who they are. They're really old. She's not dead yet in the picture, though, which means he must be even older now. His mouth is pretty much a line, but you can tell from his eyes, underneath his big woolly eyebrows, that he's happy. Also, he's standing up tall with his shoulders back and staring straight at the camera. Mrs. X has her head against his chest, smiling and happy. The way she has her arms around his waist and he has his arm around her shoulder makes them look teenager-y.

"Dinnertime!" Mom calls.

Which is a relief, because I really wasn't ready to be pathetic. Looking at Mr. X's living room makes me feel sad for him. It's full of old, dead stuff because I'm pretty sure that dog is dead now, too, along with Mrs. X, and the BVM. Dead, dead, dead.

"Bye, BVM, and dog, and Mrs. X," I whisper.

Pookie is waiting for me at the kitchen door. "Did you talk to him?"

"No. Just his pictures. He has a BVM and lots of dog—"

"You're not supposed to talk to the stupid pictures, dork," she hisses, "you're supposed to talk to the old man!"

"He wasn't there," I hiss back.

"What's wrong?" Mom says as she puts the salad on the table.

"Nothing," we both say.

Mom looks like she's going to ask another question, so I decide to deflect. "Why don't we meet at my telescope after dinner and I'll show you—"

"Not tonight, kiddo," Joan says. "I have to go to the station."

I raise my eyebrows at Mom.

"I need to look up easements and property laws," she says.

I steal a glance at Pookie.

She snorts. "Dream on."

I sigh. "Maybe we could plan to have a telescope session tomorrow night?"

Pookie rolls her eyes, which at least means she heard me. Mom and Joan start talking as if I never even said anything.

"We need a lawyer," Joan says. "We've got to fight this."

I put my fork down because tomatoes in my stomach would

not be good right now. I already feel bad and sickish for Mr. X because he's an old man, and a sad one, and he wants to die.

"We don't know how long this will take," Mom says, "so in the meantime I intend to continue fixing up the place so we can rent out rooms and run our B&B."

"I'll try to get maximum hours at the station," Joan says, "and I can also look into getting work as a physical therapist."

Mom's eyes flash. "When are you going to fit that in? We'll hardly see you."

"Well," says Pookie, "pretty soon you won't be seeing me at all because I'll be at drama camp." She puts her chocolate milk glass down dramatically. "You guys can figure this out for yourselves."

Mom and Joan look at each other, and Mom clears her throat.

Uh-oh.

"Honey, we can't afford . . . We're going to have to cancel drama camp."

"What!"

"Just for now. Until we know what's happening."

"This is so unfair! My dad would send me to drama camp!"

"I'm sure he would," Joan mutters.

"Maybe by the end of the summer—" Mom starts, but Pookie interrupts her.

"Maybe by the end of the summer I'll be gone!" She gets up from the bench so wildly she almost knocks me off. "I hate you! I hate all of you! And I hope that old man dies!" she yells as she storms up the back stairs.

The rest of the meal is pretty quiet. I'm not hungry, anyway.

Mom wipes her eyes as she walks me to my tree room to watch me climb up. I can feel her upset-ness. "Maybe you can find a camp for Pookie that's free."

She combs my hair with her fingers and smiles but doesn't say anything. I know why. It's the kind of smile that's holding the crying inside.

"Don't worry, Mom. Something magical will happen. Everything will work out."

She nods, but I can tell she doesn't believe me. That's OK, because I'm not sure I believe me, either.

If we can't make money from the B&B and Joan can't make enough for us to live on then Mom will have to go back to work except she can't because she's too freaked about that baby dying even though it wasn't her fault. But now she says she'll never deliver a baby again or be a doctor, which is too bad because she went to medical school as a grown-up and still owes a lot of money, which Joan can't afford to pay.

So I guess Mom will have to work at McDonald's, like around the clock 24/7, and I'll have to go to real middle school and Pookie will freak that we're stuck in this deadwater and everyone will be stressed.

This situation could go on for a long time. I might never get them to focus on the Dog Star. Then it'll be too late.

I take some deep breaths because that's what you're supposed to do when you feel panicky. It stops you from passing out. I also think about the universe because that usually calms me down. I start counting the Messier Objects, but when I get to M31, the

Andromeda Galaxy, I can't help thinking about how my family and Mr. X are like Andromeda and the Milky Way—two different galaxies whirling around on their own, minding their own business, until they try to occupy the same space and then they collide.

FART!

WHEN GALAXIES COLLIDE:
ANDROMEDA VERSUS THE MILKY WAY

It's going to happen. Our galaxy, the Milky Way, and the closest other galaxy to us, Andromeda, are already heading toward each other, which in most models has Earth flung into deep space, and that is NOT a good cosmic phenomenon.

There is no winner.

I don't want that to happen with us and Mr. X.

I have to stop it.

I stay awake a long time and finally try meditating, but that doesn't help, either. When I meditate I see things. I know that's not what's supposed to happen. You're supposed to clear your mind and see nothing, but that's not how it works for me. It's different from seeing normal things. Instead, I see things that aren't there. Or maybe they are. I'm pretty sure nobody else sees them, though.

Here's what I see:

Joan carries a clear medical supply bag full of whiskey bottles, some empty, some half-full. I know it's whiskey because I saw some at the ABC liquor store when I got lost at the strip mall and went in every store looking for Mom. I only got as far as the whiskey aisle because the manager pushed me out of there fast, saying it was no place for a kid, which was fine with me because it smelled like a mix of bathroom cleaner and puke.

Anyway, I don't know why Joan is carrying whiskey bottles around with her. She doesn't even drink.

Mom carries a Target shopping bag full of weird stuff, most of which doesn't belong in a Target shopping bag: her diploma, expired coupons, empty bottles of Tums, hospital baby blankets, the book she used to read to me about grandparents dying even though I never knew my grandparents, and other stuff I can't see. And she feels guilty because the bag is plastic.

Pookie's bag is not actually a bag. It's a cauldron like witches have. And the weird thing (I know, the cauldron is pretty weird already) is that it's empty. It's still heavy, though, because it's made out of cast iron and Pookie has to stoop over with her head down and arms crossed to carry it, which is how she walks in real life, too.

I don't know what Mr. X's sack looks like, but I can feel his sadness. It's a heavy gray blanket weighing me down. Also, it makes my throat hurt. Mr. X is all alone. He doesn't have Mrs. X or even his dog. Sometimes I want to be alone because it can get really noisy in our house, but I wouldn't want to be alone permanently. That would be worse than being dead.

9

MR. X

I feel like I'll never get to sleep, but I finally do and how I know is this: I have the drowning dream again.

I wake up gasping for air and also scared. I wish Joan were here, but she's staying at the fire station tonight to learn "the scoop." I don't want to wake Mom up or she'll get all upset. And Pookie would just make me feel worse.

I climb down from my tree room to look through my telescope because that always calms me down. But just as I'm walking to my telescope, Mr. X's porch light comes on.

Good. I'd really like to talk to someone right now.

I walk over to his patio and stare in the glass door. The only light I see is a dim glow from the kitchen. I can see the edge of a refrigerator. Maybe he's getting a midnight snack like I catch Joan doing. A lot. We have a deal: Joan won't tell Mom I had another nightmare if I don't tell Mom that Joan eats peanut butter straight from the jar.

I'm still squinting through the glass when I hear a rumbly noise behind me and I freeze.

"Can I help you?"

I whirl around and he's standing there. Mr. X. And I was right. He's even older than in the picture. Pookie might get her wish about him not living much longer.

"Um. Hi. I'm Julian. From next door."

His head juts forward and he squints at me. He still has big woolly eyebrows, but they're white now. He also has hair coming out of his nose, which has got to be really itchy.

"Isn't it a little dark to go sailing?" he says.

"I'm not going sailing. I'd never even get *in* a boat!"

He cocks his head at me. "Then why are you wearing a life jacket?"

"Because I don't want to die."

He swallows hard and I see the Adam's apple in his throat. "We're all going to die, kid."

"I know that, but I'm not ready yet."

"I got news for you. I'm going to die a lot sooner than you are."

"Why? What's wrong with you?"

"I'm old. That's what's wrong with me."

"Oh. Other than old, is there anything else wrong with you?"

"Why? Are you hoping I'll die off and you can keep that addition on your house?"

"No! I never said that. That was Pookie."

"Pookie?"

"My sister. But she says mean stuff all the time. She doesn't really want you to die. Probably."

"Gee, thanks. What kind of a name is Pookie, anyway?"

"It's a nickname. I'm pretty sure I was calling her Poopie because she was the one who potty trained me but everyone thought I was saying Pookie, which is a good thing because if she knew I was calling her Poopie I probably wouldn't be alive today."

People usually laugh when I tell them that story, but not Mr. X. He just looks sad. And he doesn't speak. At all. I have this thing where I have to fill in any gaps in the conversation even if it's pointless stuff. The big vacuum of silence feels too much like falling into a black hole, so I spew random words.

"My name's Julian."

"You said that already."

"Oh. I was named after Percy Lavon Julian. Do you know who he was?"

Mr. X shakes his head.

"It's OK, most people don't. I'll tell you—and I'll also tell you why a lot of people don't know his name." I walk over to the glider chair on his patio and sit down.

"Make yourself at home."

"Thanks. At home, Mom makes me chocolate milk."

"I was being sarcastic."

"Oh. OK, I'll just tell you about Mr. Julian, then."

He sinks down on the bench with a puffy cushion on it, and the air hisses out of him just like it hisses out of the cushion. "I'm so lucky," he mutters.

"Percy Lavon Julian was this chemist who made all kinds of life-saving products like the foam in fire extinguishers and a bunch of stuff out of soybeans like hormones used to fight cancer and cortisone that stops pain. He could've done a lot more, too, except that he was African American back when people were stupid so he had to waste a lot of time finding a school that would take him and then a job that would take him and then a lab that would let him experiment. Isn't that crazy? Just think what he could've done if people had just let him be brilliant! He might actually have cured cancer or terrible heart problems or done something else amazing!"

Mr. X doesn't seem to understand how incredible Mr. Julian was.

"Don't you see? In spite of everything he left the world a much better place. I want to be like that, too. People say, *His legacy lives on*. That means we still use the discoveries he made. Even though people don't know his name, they're grateful for all the stuff he did—lots of stuff. Percy Lavon Julian saved people he didn't even *know* and weren't even born until after he died! That's magic!"

I realize I'm standing up now because Mr. X is leaning back in his seat to get away from me.

"You get pretty worked up over this, don't you, kid?"

"It's a big responsibility to be named after him."

"It's just a name."

"Yeah, a name that's going on a comet!"

I'm not sure if he actually says he doesn't understand or I'm just uni-sensing it.

"I'm going to find a comet and name it Julian and then I can live forever."

Mr. X shakes his head.

"You don't believe me?"

He shrugs. "You can't live forever. It's impossible."

"No, it's not. It's physics. Conservation of matter. Nothing disappears; it just changes form."

"Sure, kid," he whispers, and I notice he's looking through his patio doors, into the living room, straight at the picture of him and Mrs. X and he's swallowing hard.

"I'm really sorry about your wife, but she's still around and you can talk to her."

He whips his head back to me.

"It's OK to talk to people who aren't right here. It's like talking with an imaginary friend or a friend in a parallel universe."

He tries to say something but no words come out and he has to snuff up and blink, which gives me more time to say the stuff he needs to hear.

"I used to have friends in parallel universes all the time. Rudy was my favorite. He got to do all the stuff I wasn't allowed to, like ride his bike in the driveway without his mom holding on to the handlebars, and go to summer camp outside of his own house, and eat marshmallows for breakfast. My therapist said it's a good way to talk through your anxiety and—"

Mr. X holds up his hand. "Stop!"

But I don't. "Your wife was real and lived right here in this universe so it's even more normal to talk with her. It helps, I know, because Mom—"

He stands up so fast he almost knocks the cushion off his bench. "I have to go now. I'm not comfortable talking with you."

"That's OK, you'll get comfortable because I'm going to be right here."

"Do you always talk to strangers?" he snaps.

"No. Only if I need to."

He points to our house. "To try and stop me from taking down that addition?"

"No, because you need a friend. And so do I. But this time I think I'm doing it more for you than for me."

He stares at me, and when it starts turning into more of a glare I know that's my cue to leave.

"See ya, Mr. X," I say and go to my telescope to look for comets but also Mimas.

"Mr. X." I hear him snort but he doesn't argue so I guess he likes his name OK.

FART!

MIMAS

Mimas is a moon of Saturn that is too small to see with my telescope so I don't know why I'm thinking about it. Mimas looks like the Death Star. No, really. It has a big bite taken out of it. Something collided with it and made a huge crater so it still orbits Saturn but it wobbles a lot. Astronomers think it's either filled with water or it's football-shaped inside. we don't know for sure but what's clear, if you have the right telescope, is its wound.

And now I know why Mr. X made me think of Mimas.

10

UNI-SENSING

The next morning, Pookie wakes me up, which is not the best way to wake up.

"Get down here, squirt! I'm not waiting all day. Next time, Mom can come watch her precious baby get down from the tree alive."

"So-rry," I mutter, even though it's not my fault Mom thinks I need a spotter just to climb down a ladder.

"You have to try to catch our neighbor today," she says.

"I already did. I talked with him last night."

"And?"

"He's a little grump-ish but he's OK."

She rolls her eyes. "I mean, what did he say about the addition?"

"Oh. I forgot to ask him that." I didn't really forget. He felt too sad already and I didn't want to make him sadder.

"Jeez, Julian! Do I have to do everything around here?"

"You don't do anything around here."

"Shut up!"

She marches over to his patio and bangs on the glass door so loudly it makes me cringe.

He doesn't answer.

I wouldn't, either.

When we go in the kitchen, Mom tells her to change into something more presentable and Pookie narrows her eyes. She opens her mouth but then looks down at her boxers and faded World Wildlife T-shirt, turns, and stomps through the pantry up the back stairs. I think having sneaky back stairs is really cool, but Pookie probably isn't even thinking about that. She's probably still mad about drama camp.

Mom looks stressed out so I play a game we used to play when I was little. "If you could pick one superpower what would it be?"

She gives me a tired smile. "Boundless energy. How about you?"

I grin and answer how I always do. "To go back in time, to fly, and to become invisible, even though that's three."

"What would you do if you could go back in time?"

This is where I have to give a different answer. I've already said stuff like see the dinosaurs or see Mom when she was a little girl, especially if she's getting in trouble, or warn Hitler's parents that they need to change their parenting style. "I'd go back and meet Mrs. X and see when Mr. X was happy."

"Who are Mr. and Mrs. X?"

"Our neighbor. I call him Mr. X because of his funny last name and—"

"Oh, like your music teacher. I remember." She gives me a sad smile. "That's very sweet of you, honey."

"I feel bad for him. I'd like to see him when he used to be happy."

She squeezes my hand and is quiet for a moment. "OK, how about flying?"

I decide to plant a seed in her head. "I'd fly to the far edge of our Milky Way galaxy so I could see Sirius, the Dog Star, up close, instead of through my *telescope*."

Mom doesn't pick up on the hint because she moves right on to the third superpower. "And let me guess, invisible so you could spy on Pookie?"

"Sure," I say, although I'd also spy on her and Joan, like when I heard them talking about me before we moved and Mom was worried that it was a long ambulance ride to the hospital and shouldn't we live closer to a major medical facility and Joan said she should calm down or she'd pass her worry on to me so that's how I know to act like nothing bothers me.

I didn't even have to be invisible for that one. Sometimes you just get lucky.

"Julian, I'm looking for a pediatrician for you."

Asciugamano! I shouldn't have thought about that medical conversation because I sent that idea straight from my brain to hers.

Mom slams her mug down on the table and I jump. I think she's mad at me for a second until I realize she's looking past me. I turn around and see Pookie in the pantry doorway.

She's wearing a cropped T-shirt with a bra on the outside instead of the inside and her shorts that say EAST-ERN on the butt, which Mom hates, with the waistband rolled down so far you can see her underpants.

Mom is clenching her teeth.

Pookie smirks. "Isn't it cool? And when we go to Italy for squirt to . . . do whatever it is he wants to go to Italy for—"

"See the Leaning Tower of Pisa," I remind her, "where Galileo—"

"Then," she cuts me off, "we can visit the fashion capitol, Milan."

"It's not Milan," I say, "it's Milano."

"Milano is a cookie, stupid."

"It was a city first."

Mom has unclenched her teeth because she's talking now. Loudly. "You are not wearing that outfit in public!"

"If he can wear a life jacket and British pants, I can express myself, too!"

"That's different! Your outfit is indecent!"

"My dad would let me wear this!"

After that, the argument gets louder but I block my ears and quietly get up from the table and go out the kitchen door.

I'm about to climb up to my room when Mom comes running outside. "Julian! Remember to always tell someone when you're using the ladder."

Pookie stands in the kitchen doorway, rolling her eyes. "He wears that stupid life jacket all the time. He'd probably bounce."

"He would not bounce!"

"Seriously, Mom, why don't you put a helmet on him and wrap him in sofa cushions and be done with it?"

"Don't start on that—"

I'm up in my room now so I can cover my ears and not have to hear any more. My stomach acid is already churning like a mini tsunami.

When Mom and Pookie go back inside I uncover my ears but I can still hear them, so I decide to pedal my stationary bike because it makes its own noise until I hear Pookie slam her Jill door, several times, and I know the arguing is over, for now.

I go back up to my tree room and I guess since I was awake a lot last night I actually fall asleep. I wake up kind of groggy. From my room I can see that Pookie is lying on the dock, Mom's car is gone, and so is Joan's, so she must still be at the station.

And I see Mr. X sitting on his patio. I go down the ladder, run over to him, and sit on the glider chair. "Hi, it's me again."

"Hi, you again."

He's not smiling. It doesn't feel like he's mad, just sad. So I tell him what he needs to hear. "My mom talks to my grandfather all the time and he's dead. *Death cannot stop true love.* That's what Westley says in *The Princess Bride*, remember?"

"What's *The Princess Bride*?"

"Only the best movie of all time! It was a book first, but in this case the movie is as good as the book."

"Never heard of it."

"Inconceivable! That's a line from the movie. *Inconceivable* means something is so unbelievable it couldn't possibly happen but actually the guy who says it is wrong because it does happen."

Mr. X stares at me.

I shrug. "Sometimes things seems impossible but actually they're not."

He still looks confused.

"We have it on DVD, so you can watch it with me."

He shakes his head. "I'm not a princess movie kind of guy."

"It's not a princess movie. It's a swashbuckling adventure. You'll see. And it has a grandfather in it, too. I think he's a lot like mine was."

Mr. X clears his throat. "Look, I'm sorry about your grandfather, kid, but I—"

"Me too. I only got to see him once. When I was born. But I remember him."

"Sure you do."

"No, really. I almost died when I was born so I think we passed each other, only I came back and he didn't. I think it's how I got uni-sensory perception."

He doesn't ask me what uni-sensory perception is, which most people do, but he's probably wondering so I tell him.

"Uni-sensory perception is sensing the universe. It's not exactly hearing or seeing or feeling, it's more like getting a sense of something, not in the regular way but a magical way. It's like picking up on nonverbal cues. For example, right now you're kind of annoyed with me even though you're not saying it."

Mr. X makes his grumbly sound.

"Anyway, my grandfather told me three things when we passed each other: the world is a magical place, he loves me very much, and take care of my mom and sister. That was before Joan came along, but I'm sure he would've said to take care of her, too, even though Joan is pretty good at taking care of herself."

Mr. X is staring at me.

"I think he told me one more thing as he passed but I'm not sure. I think it was, *Never burn your marshmallows.*"

Mr. X squints his eyes at me like he can't quite believe I'm real.

"It could be true because once when we were making s'mores I burned my marshmallow and I said, *Sorry, Granddad*, and Mom just about went orbital because she said the one thing he couldn't stand was the smell of burned marshmallows."

Mr. X still doesn't say anything so I have to fill the black hole of silence.

"I also remember what my grandfather looked like. Pookie says I only know because I've seen pictures of him, but she's wrong. I knew what he looked like before that. I uni-sensed him. Nobody except Mom believes me, and I'm not even sure she really believes me. She just wants to believe me. But it's true."

Mr. X pinches his nose. That's what grown-ups do when they want to pick their nose but they're in public. "Uh-huh, so your grandfather talked to you as you were being born." He definitely sounds like he doesn't believe me.

"Actually, he didn't talk to me. It's uni-sensing. Like a Vulcan mind meld on *Star Trek.*"

He makes his rumbly grumbling sound.

"I know. *Star Trek* is just a movie, but it was a TV show before it was a movie, and in this case the books came after. But stuff that seemed impossible on *Star Trek* when it first came out is now real, like tricorders and talking computers and even the holodeck. Maybe even tractor beams. So just because we don't understand something now doesn't mean it's not true or real. It only means we're too stupid at the moment. Anyway, the point is Mrs. X can still—"

"Julian."

I stop because he's actually saying my name instead of *kid*. "What?"

"No more talking about my wife."

"But if you—"

"None. Understand?"

"Not really. I understand you're upset, but if you'd just listen—"

He makes that grumbling sound in his throat. Really loud. Like a space shuttle taking off.

"OK. I guess that's enough for today. I'll be back, though."

"You don't give up, do you?"

I shake my head. "It took physicists forty-eight years to find the Higgs boson—that's a tiny, tiny particle, smaller than an atom or quarks even—but they knew it had to exist so they kept looking until they found it. That's how come I'm not giving up on finding a comet. I believe it's there. I believe my grandfather is out there, too, even though I can't see him now. And I believe that your . . . the lady I'm not supposed to mention who used to live in this house . . . is still around, too."

Mr. X pinches his nose again and makes his throaty grumbly sound so I leave, but after a few steps I turn back again.

"I know I can be annoying sometimes but it's for a good cause."

He looks confused, like he doesn't know what the good cause is.

It's him! It's to show him the magic of the universe again. He thinks all the magic went out of life when his wife died. I have to show him that's not true.

Mr. X may not realize he needs me, but I do. I can always uni-sense when people need me.

That night, I'm staring up at the full moon and noticing how it lights up everything and I think about how I don't need my flashlight but my family does so I decide to bring it to them. Someone's still awake because there's a light on in the kitchen. Probably Joan. I know it seems weird to bring my family a flashlight when there's already a light on in the kitchen, but I've learned not to question my uni-sensing even if I don't understand it right away.

When I get to the kitchen door I see it's Pookie making chocolate milk, not Joan eating peanut butter. I can see through the window part of the door that she has a glass of milk and is looking in the fridge for the syrup.

I open the door and Pookie whirls around.

"Jeez, don't sneak up on me like that!"

"I wasn't. I'm just bringing you guys a flashlight."

"We don't need a flash—"

Right then, the lights go out.

Pookie doesn't say anything, but once our eyes adjust to the dark I can see she's glaring at me.

Part of me wants to say, *Told ya*, but I'm not stupid. I just say it with my eyes, which annoys her even more. I know because when she grabs the flashlight out of my hand she makes a really loud orangutan noise, even though she uses the flashlight to find the chocolate syrup because otherwise she wouldn't be able to see. I'm still standing there when she stomps through the pantry with her milk, goes up the stairs, and slams her Jill door.

FART!

UNI-SENSING

Pookie used to think it was cool that I was a uni-sensor, like knowing her bus broke down and making Mom pick her up even though Mom kept staring at me and asking me how I knew. Or checking out three books at the library that weren't even on comets (they were on costumes through the ages) even though Mom looked at them funny, and I did, too, but it turns out Pookie needed them for a report that was due the next day. Or feeling that Pookie was having a really bad day and fixing two glasses of chocolate milk, pulling out her Matt Damon DVDs, and dragging the stuffed kiddie sofa in front of the TV and

when she got home she said I was the best
brother in the whole universe.

After that she left our universe, but I'm still
uni-sensing her and everyone else.

It's how I know Granddad and Mrs. X are up
there in the stars. And Granddad has Mom to
talk to him, but no one is talking to Mrs. X. She
needs Mr. X. She's probably scared and feeling all
alone. When I figure out what star she's in I'm
going to tell her that I'll get Mr. X to start
talking to her really soon.

I wake up and it's still dark but I can see just fine like there's a
really bright streetlamp next to my tree room lighting up the
house and yard and lake. It's the moon. I can't believe how bright it
is! And the stars are popping like LEDs! It seems like a dream
only it's not. It's like an out-of-body experience and it's very
exciting and awesome and if this is what it's like to live in the stars
I think it'll be OK. I lie back down and look at Orion as if I'm seeing it from Sirius and it looks pretty cool from there, too.

MAGIC

I walk in the kitchen for breakfast and Mom practically drops her coffee mug. "Joan!"

"What?" Joan says, without looking up from the papers that are spread across the table.

"It was your turn to see that Julian got down from that tree safely!"

"Oh, look," says Joan, her voice deadpan, "he's down safely."

"But—"

"Whoop-whoop-whoop-whoop-whoop," Joan says. "The kiddo is—"

"I'm not being helicopter-ish, Joan, I'm concerned—"

"Michelle, he's almost ten. The platform is less than ten feet off the ground. And he's wearing a life jacket. He'd probably bounce."

I hear Pookie snort from the back stairs.

Mom glares at Joan.

"I'm fine, Mom," I say quickly. "Did you know that if you do too much for children it robs them of their self-esteem? You're sending the message that they can't cope and they start internalizing it."

Mom glares at me now. "Have you been reading my parenting books again?"

"Well, they're about me, aren't they?"

Joan smirks.

"How do you know they're not about me?" Pookie says, strutting into the kitchen and turning her head back and forth so we can see that she shaved the back except for the gelled piece that sticks out like a spike.

"Whoa! Cool! You look anime, Pookie!"

She actually smiles. "What do you think, Joan?"

"Fine by me," Joan says, looking back at her papers.

Pookie's teeth clench. "Mom?"

I notice Joan's eyes slide sideways to look at Mom. Mom notices, too.

"It's . . . fine, honey, if . . . that's what you want."

Pookie frowns. "I'm also thinking of getting my nose and tongue pierced. And a tattoo."

Nobody says anything. Probably because we all know that Pookie can't stand needles, and the only thing she can't stand more than needles is any kind of pain.

She makes her orangutan noise and stomps into the pantry, yelling, "Nobody in this family cares about me!"

Mom looks up at the ceiling. "Oh, Dad, I wish you were still here."

I think it's cool that Mom talks to Granddad. I wish Mr. X would talk with Mrs. X so he could feel better. And so would she. That's when it hits me. Like a comet piercing the sky. I know just what Mr. X needs.

I run through the pantry to go to my room, not my tree room but the upstairs room, Jack. I almost trip over Pookie, who's sitting at the bottom of the stairs. "Sorry!"

"Watch it, squirt! Where are you going, anyway?"

"To Jack!"

"Oh, jeez, are you back to imaginary friends again?" she yells.

"Leave him alone," Mom calls from the kitchen. "There's nothing wrong with talking things out with someone, even if that someone is imaginary."

"Jack, the *room*," I call down the stairs, but I don't know if they hear me. I don't care, anyway, I'm on a mission. For a real friend.

Hi, Mr. X,

It's me. Julian. From next door.

I'm writing to you because some subjects are easier to write since it's too awkward to talk about unless you're in a car and the grown-up has to look at the road and you can look out the side window and no one has to see anyone's face.

I'm really sorry about your wife and I know it's hard for you to talk about so I'm giving you my book about death. Now you can read it and maybe it'll help you.* It helped Mom. She read it to me like a kajillion times and I know it by heart. I think she was reading it for herself, anyway, because I didn't even know my grandfather that well since he died the day I was born. I just know what he said about the universe being magic, and that he loved me, and to take care of Mom and Pookie. And maybe not to burn marshmallows but I'm still not 100 percent sure about that one.

The best page is the one that's wrinkled because that's where Mom always cried but she said she felt better afterward. Mom stopped reading the book to me years ago so she obviously doesn't need it anymore. That's because she TALKS to Granddad instead. Remember that it's OK to talk to people who aren't around because they're here, really, just in another form. They never actually leave us, which is pretty magical when you think about it. They're in the stars. So is Mrs. X. You really need to talk to her. If you don't, she's going to be awful lonely. She misses you.**

Your friend,
Julian***

*I bet you're thinking, "What does a kid know about death, anyway?" but I do know how you feel, sort of. To me, talking about swimming is like talking about death. So let's not talk about it. It's OK, anyway, because I wear my life jacket all the time. Mom would freak if she knew the real reason. Even Joan would be worried. Joan acts like nothing bothers her but she worries about stuff, too. I know because she stress eats a LOT.

**Remember that she can see you so stop pinching your nose. It looks like you're picking it.

Isn't it cool how your wife's name, Julia, is almost the same as mine only you add an n? Like the n factor in math?*

****The n in math stands for something that's variable, which means it can change.*****

*****Change can be hard but it's also a good thing. Like making a new friend. Which would be really good for you right now. And for me.

I put the package at his front door in case it rains because the patio doesn't have any covering. Now that I've taught Mr. X something, it's time to work on my own family.

I spend all morning making custom star charts showing where in the sky the Dog Star is. If I can't get my family to look through my telescope, I can at least give them each a cheat sheet. Maybe they'll learn something before they even realize it. That's what happened when Pookie went to *The Martian* movie because Matt Damon was in it. Now she thinks Mars is cool. Only Mars, she says, but it's a start. Thanks, Matt Damon!

When I'm done, I fold over each chart and personalize the outsides. On Pookie's, I write, "Important Fashion Information!" and on Joan's, "New Paramedic Regulations!" and on Mom's, "How to Beat the Winter Blues!"

This past February, I set up my telescope inside by the living room window so Mom wouldn't have to go out in the cold. She loved it. And she had to admit I was right that the sky is beautiful no matter how gloomy the days are. She was amazed when she saw the Dog Star. I told her it was the brightest star in our galaxy and she smiled and said, "Just like you."

That's when I knew I wanted to be in the Dog Star forever so Mom could always see me even in the worst month with the darkest days, and be happy.

FART!

STAR STUFF

I'd like to find which star Mrs. X is in so I can tell Mr. X, but I need to learn more about her first. All I really know is that she died of cancer. So maybe she's in the constellation Cancer? There are a lot of stars in Cancer, including two star clusters that are Messier Objects (M_{44} and M_{67}). M_{44} is the only one I can pronounce because it's in English: the Beehive Cluster. Cancer must be pretty full since that's how a lot of people die. I hope they're having a huge party up there with lots of marshmallows.

On the other hand, my grandfather died of a heart attack, which is how I almost died even though I was a baby because it was a heart condition not an old person's kind of heart attack, but there's no heart constellation I've heard of. I'm pretty sure he's in the Wild Duck Cluster of stars because Mom says he liked ducks a LOT.

Once I name a comet I'll be in all the science books and websites and everyone will remember me. If I don't find a comet, which I will but even if I don't, at least I'll be in Sirius so I can watch over my family and they can see me, too. I just hope they read their star charts before then.

12

BEEHIVE CLUSTER

I haven't seen Mr. X for a few days. I hope he's not mad at me for sending him the death letter. If he is I hope he gets over it soon because I miss having someone to talk to. I can't talk to anyone in my family. They are super massively stressed. Even Joan. I think Joan asked to work extra hours on purpose. The only times she's home is when I'm already asleep.

None of them say anything to me about their star charts.

Mom's is in a pile of papers on her desk.

Joan's is probably in her Outback because that's where she puts a lot of her stuff so Mom doesn't have to rant about how messy she is and Joan doesn't have to hear it.

I find Pookie's star chart crumpled up in the trash.

Ever since Pookie heard she can't go to drama camp she has been making up for it by acting out her own drama camp right here. Mom is so tense she jumps when you say her name, even if you say it in the quiet yoga way and not the scream-y Pookie way.

This morning I told Mom she should be meditating regularly

and she snapped at me, saying, "Are *you* meditating regularly?" and when I said yes she was even crankier.

I haven't actually been meditating, but at least I've thought about it. I read that when you think about doing something your brain goes through the motions almost like you're actually doing it so I was almost telling the truth when I said I'm meditating.

I look at Pookie down by the lake. She says the only saving grace about this deadwater is the lake and now that we're poor and have to move she won't even have the water part, just the dead.

I think it's an excuse to lie on the dock, which is her new Moody Place, and not do any work. I wish Mom wouldn't let her get away with it. If Joan were back from her thirty-six-hour shift at the station Pookie wouldn't try this because Joan won't put up with the princess crap, only she uses another word that means the same thing.

Mom and I work on house projects together, like painting the porch railings and fence, planting tomatoes out back, and planting flowers in front. It's not exactly quality time. Even when I talk she's not listening. When I ask her a question like when can I show her Sirius she says, *I don't know* or, *Later*, or even, *That's nice*. It's like talking into the vacuum of deep space or to a thirteen-year-old. It's the way Pookie acted after she left being normal (twelve) and before she became a galactic nightmare (fourteen).

Pookie comes in from the dock just as I'm finishing sweeping the porch and flops on one of the lounge chairs.

"Hey! You're tracking sand! I already swept that part."

"Get me my earbuds, squirt."

"Why?"

She rolls her eyes. "Because I need them. Duh!"

Mom pushes the screen door open and sticks her head out. "Oh, there you are, Pookie." She says it like she's actually happy to see her. "Would you mind helping me with—"

"I have a headache!" Pookie yells and lies back on the lounge chair, groaning.

Mom sighs. "OK. Can I get you anything?"

"A strawberry kiwi smoothie. And," she says, glaring at me, "I need my earbuds."

Mom stays calm, which is pretty good for Mom. "Maybe later, when you're feeling better, you can—"

"I can what? Do more work for you like an enslaved person? Jeez!"

Mom squishes her lips together and goes back inside.

"That's all I am to them," Pookie mutters, "an enslaved person."

I'm not an expert on enslaved persons, but I'm pretty sure they don't get to skip work just by faking a headache, or lie on the porch while someone makes them a strawberry kiwi smoothie, or order someone to get their earbuds for them so they can listen to music on their phone.

She glares at her phone. "I don't even have a data plan!"

She doesn't have a data plan because Mom and Joan cut her off after she did something really bad on the Internet, and I don't know what it was but it had to do with finding her dad. They said she couldn't have Internet back until she can use it in a positive way. Basically, that means when she stops being the dark energy that's sucking up the entire universe.

"Pookie, if you weren't in such a bad mood—"

"This is not about me, stupid!" She sighs. "It's never about me."

What is she even talking about? It's always about her! "How come you're so mad all the time?"

She pulls her sunglasses down enough to glare at me. "You really don't get it, do you? You're, like, from another planet. Maybe that's why you love your telescope so much."

Mom turns the blender on and I remember that she and Joan got me my telescope when Pookie went supernova and wouldn't spend time with me anymore. And then I think of something— what if Pookie is jealous of my telescope? And how I don't spend time with her anymore? I never thought of that!

"Do you want to look through it tonight?"

"No, I don't want to look through your telescope." She turns to me and even though the blender is pulsing I hear her loud and clear. "I'm not part of your universe anymore, and the sooner you accept that the better."

"We used to be best friends, remember?"

"That's over."

"Why?"

She rolls her eyes. "You're so clueless."

"Then tell me!" I yell over the blender noise. "Please?"

The blender stops and everything is still. For a second, Pookie looks like she's going to talk to me the way she used to, but then she shakes her head. "You wouldn't understand."

"Yes, I would. I'm not stupid."

She throws her head back and laughs.

I stare at her for a minute and when she finally looks at my face she stops laughing. "No offense, squirt, but—"

I yank the screen door open just in time for Mom to come through with her smoothie. "Thanks, honey." She doesn't even notice how mad I am, that my heart is practically pushing itself out of my chest and then there'll be this empty hole in there where the nice Pookie used to be.

Mom follows me into the kitchen. "Can you get her earbuds, honey?"

"Really?" Pookie's glare must be contagious, because I'm giving one to Mom.

She sighs. "Julian, I'm just trying to make her happy."

"You can't make people happy, Mom. They have to find the happiness in themselves."

She smiles even though her eyes are drooping. "You are so smart."

"Not really. We learned that in yoga class, remember?"

"Oh. Right. Honey, you've done enough work for today. Why don't you take a break?" She sighs again. "I'll get Pookie's earbuds for her."

I wish it were dark so I could see the cosmos now and calm down because I'm kind of annoyed. Instead, I ride my bike really fast and hard for seven miles, which is supposedly a lucky number but it doesn't feel lucky, just sore legs on the outside and still annoyed on the inside. Why can't my family even get their act together enough to look through a telescope? *Asciugamano!*

I go up to my tree room and fill in my chart of Messier Objects, including the Beehive Cluster (M_{44}). I've found almost two-thirds of the Messier Objects now, although not necessarily in order. It helps calm me down a little bit to record them all.

I'm just writing down M_{74}, a galaxy in the constellation Pisces, when I hear a splash, and even though I don't like looking at the lake, I can't help it. What's weird is that a bunch of fish are jumping and splashing in the water. They dance from the middle of the lake to the other side. Why would they do that? And how come I've never noticed it before? And how come I only noticed it when I was writing down M_{74}, Pisces, which means fish?

I stare across the lake and see the GROTTO WITH BVM gas station sign, just barely. An eagle flies past the sign, or I think it's an eagle, anyway, which reminds me that I forgot to record M_{16}, the Eagle Nebula. I fill it in, thinking how cool it is that I just saw an eagle when a butterfly lands right on my page. And guess where it lands? On M_6. The Butterfly Cluster.

FART!

COINCIDENCE VERSUS MAGIC

People always say things are just a coincidence and it's silly to believe it's anything more than that. They even say if scientists can't explain things, then they're not real. But just because we can't explain something doesn't mean it's not real. Maybe we just don't understand it yet, and someday we will. And then we'll understand how I know when my sister's upset even though she's somewhere else, or to get my family a flashlight before the electricity goes out, or that my grandfather told me he loves me even though I was just being born.

Whatever it is, you shouldn't ignore stuff like that. It's your brain trying to show you the magic. If you keep ignoring it, it'll get tired of showing you the magic and you'll end up not seeing it anymore, just like my family. And Mr. X.

What I notice next is not so magical. It's Pookie. Back in the water. I guess her headache has miraculously gone away. She keeps bending down, picking up rocks from under the water, staring at them, and hurling them toward the house. Like the Oort Cloud flinging comets from the outer solar system toward Earth, trying to whack us.

I really want to talk with Mr. X again. I peek in from his patio but he's not there, so I walk around his house just in case he's out front. I even ring his doorbell and knock on the front door, which I normally never do because, like I said, it reminds me of Halloween, not in a good way but a scary way. Even nice people dress up and try to scare kids on Halloween, and every time I press a doorbell I think of our neighbor in DC who was nice except on Halloween when he wore this creepy mask and jumped at you, screaming. I don't know why kids thought it was funny. Well, not all of them. If you were under six, or me, then you were scared.

There's no answer at his door so I walk down his front stairs and that's when I notice his garage. It's like a little house with double doors and windows too high for me to see through. There's something shut doors or closed boxes or sealed envelopes do to me: They make me want to open them. It's like a magnetic attraction and I can't stop myself. I know I shouldn't open them but I have a heightened sense of responsibility most of the time so sometimes it's OK to let myself be a regular kid.

When I open Mr. X's garage door and look inside, my stomach gets instantly queasy. There's no car in the garage. Instead, it's a boat.

I stare at it without getting close to it. Why would he have a boat? I mean, I know he lives by a lake, but isn't he too old to go in the lake? What if he drowned? It's too dangerous.

"What do you think?" Mr. X asks, and I whirl around to see him.

"I don't like boats. They make me seasick."

"This is just a little thing. Touch it."

"No, thanks."

"It won't make you sick if you touch it. But don't bang on it or you might break it."

Now he's just teasing me and I glare at him.

"I'm serious. It's made of Styrofoam." He points to some big chunks of Styrofoam and a box that says FIBERGLASS CLOTH next to the boat. "I made it myself."

"A boat? Made out of Styrofoam? Who would use something like that? In the water? That's crazy!"

"It's seaworthy. It's covered in fiberglass cloth, but you still don't want to gouge it. It's so lightweight you could drag it to the water yourself and row across—"

"No way!"

"It's easy to row a boat."

"I know how to row. I used the rowing machine at Joan's old firehouse a kajillion times."

He rolls his eyes. "Oh, like you know how to ride a bike."

I stare at him. "I do ride a bike."

He snorts. "A stationary bike."

"So?"

"Tight leash," he mutters, which is what Joan always says.

They can say what they want, but a stationary bike you can ride in the middle of the night or with your eyes closed, so it's even better than a real bike. Just like a rowing machine is better than a real boat. Then you don't have to get in the water.

"Maybe I'll get you out in it some day."

"Are you kidding? I wouldn't be caught dead in that thing. I wouldn't be caught alive in it, either."

I shouldn't have said *dead* because now he looks all sad again. He pinches his nose and stares at the boat so I look at it, too. And that's when I see it, on the side of the boat. BEEHIVE. It must be

Mrs. X! He must've named this boat after her because that's what people do with boats.

"Beehive!" I can't help saying it out loud. I even touch the boat and feel the fiberglass coating. And lift it a little bit because I'm curious that way. It really is light. I turn to Mr. X. "Did you seriously call her Beehive?"

He shrugs. "It was a nickname. The first time I saw her she had a beehive hairdo."

He looks over at a framed photo on the wall that I guess is Mrs. X when she was a LOT younger. Her hair is piled on top of her head in a giant bun and someone drew little bees buzzing around it and wrote across the top, "My Beehive."

"Do you know what's amazing?" I ask him. "I was looking at the Beehive Cluster of stars just last night!"

"Why is that amazing?"

"Because I was thinking about Mrs. X! I'm pretty sure that's where she is now!"

He sighs, but more in a sad way than a mad way. "Look, kid—"

"And you really need to talk to her so she won't be lonely. She misses you."

He swallows several times and I'm afraid he's going to cry so I say something silly. "Remember, she can always see you so make sure you're not doing anything gross like picking your nose." I grin.

He makes a little choky sound like he's swallowing his cry and letting a laugh come out instead. He looks around, blinking, until his eyes settle on the boat. He juts his chin toward it. "Maybe someday you'll try that out."

I shake my head and think of a way to deflect but I can't so I just repeat myself. "I was looking at the Beehive Cluster last night and your boat is named Beehive. Isn't that magic?"

"Coincidence."

"Or maybe it's the universe talking to us."

He shakes his head. "Coincidence."

"It's not a coincidence. Nothing is a coincidence."

"You sound like Julia. Everything happened for a reason."

"She's right!"

"Coincidence," he says again, like the conversation is over.

But it isn't.

"It's not a coincidence." I have to prove that to him. Suddenly, I have a thought. "What was your dog's name?"

He looks confused. "Which one?"

"The one you have all those pictures of. No, wait—don't tell me. I'll tell you." I think for a moment about the star cluster that comes after Beehive in the Messier Objects. Beehive is M_{44} and M_{45} is . . . "I've got it! Your dog's name was Taurus."

His eyes get wider than I've ever seen and his face gets paler. It's like I can see right through him.

Finally, he makes his rumbling sound. "I must've mentioned his name."

"No, you didn't. We've never had a conversation about your dog. I'd remember because I love dogs. And Taurus is exactly the kind of dog I want. A black Lab! See? It's the universe talking to us!"

Mr. X rolls his eyes.

"And your wife's name was Julia and my name is Julian. Isn't that amazing?"

"Not really."

"And we think the same way—you just said so yourself! We must've been thrown together for some reason, Mr. X. The universe is trying to tell us something!"

"OK, then, what's the universe saying?"

"I don't know yet."

"That's because the universe isn't talking to us."

"Maybe it is and you're just not listening! Maybe you're doing this." I close my eyes, put my hands over my ears, and go, "LA-LA-LA-LA-LA," really loudly.

As loud as I am I can hear him saying my name, several times, so I finally stop.

"I think someone's calling you."

And then I hear it, too.

Mom.

In a panic.

"*Asciugamano!* I have to go!"

13

FRIENDS

Mom is out front and grabs me in a big hug, then drags me up the stairs into the front hall like outside is too dangerous. She's crying.

"It's OK, Mom. I'm sorry, I was—"

"Julian!" Pookie comes flying in, dripping wet from the lake. "Are you OK?"

"Yes! I just didn't hear her so I didn't come right away. That's all."

For a moment Pookie actually looks relieved, and sweet, like she used to. Then she glares at Mom. "Jeez, Mom, do you have to go into a panic any time he's out of your sight? You freaked out everyone in a three-mile radius."

Mom has stopped crying and is staring Pookie up and down. "I told you not to come into this house tracking in sand. Now clean that up."

Pookie's eyes narrow. "Yes, master."

Mom takes a deep breath to let out the power of the universe so I quickly say, "What's for dinner?" I'm not even hungry but I'm deflecting.

Mom's teeth are clenched and she's still glaring at Pookie as she says, "I don't know."

I pat Mom's hand. "I know! I'll make dinner! Beans on toast. It's a British treat. Well, maybe not a treat, but it's a meal for"— I stop myself before saying *for poor people* because that might upset Mom—"for British people. And us, too."

Pookie stomps to the front porch and grabs a beach towel from the railing and cleans up her drippy spots, which is actually really good timing for her because Joan drives up and now she'll think Pookie has been working all day instead of being a princess.

"How's my family?" Joan asks, breezing into the kitchen.

Pookie stomps up the back stairs.

Mom sighs, pulling Joan toward the front porch.

"That good, huh?" Joan says.

"I'm making dinner, Joan," I call after them. "It involves beans so you'll like it."

"Thanks, kiddo!"

Beans are the only vegetable Joan will eat. She has what Mom calls a *limited palate*, which means her favorite foods are mac and cheese and hamburgers. And French fries, but she only gets those when we're out somewhere without Mom.

Mom and Joan talk quietly on the front porch and even though it's worse not knowing what people are saying than actually hearing them, I try to tell my stomach not to get upset and focus on dinner.

It's pretty easy to make beans on toast. You get the bag of green beans out of the freezer and put them in the microwave until they're soft, which is about as long as it takes to make toast because our toaster is old and tired. And maybe I burned the toast just a little. Then you pour the beans on top of the toast and you're done!

When I call everyone to dinner, Pookie takes one look at her plate and fake pukes. "Mom! Joan! We aren't really supposed to eat this, are we?"

I'm expecting Mom and Joan to roll their eyes at her, but their eyes are focused on my beans on toast.

"Julian," Joan says quietly, "I think it's supposed to be baked beans, not green beans, that go on top of toast."

"It's not even toast!" Pookie says. "It's mushy burned bread that's disintegrating in bean water!"

I look down at my plate and realize it doesn't look too appetizing. It smells weird, too.

Mom takes a bite, chews slowly, and looks thoughtful. "It's sort of like green bean casserole, without the mushroom soup or onions. I think it's fine."

Joan stares at Mom. "I think it was a good try."

"We can eat it," Mom shoots back.

Pookie pushes her plate over to Mom. "*You* can eat it!" She storms off to the back stairs again.

"Wait!" I call after her. "We can have marshmallows instead!"

"Julian," Mom says, "that's only for—"

"Special occasions, I know. This is special."

"Yes, it is," Joan says. "Get the marshmallows. Please."

The only thing better than marshmallows is marshmallows plus something else, like in s'mores, but we don't have Hershey's bars or graham crackers. It's still a pretty good dinner, though, because Mom only makes me eat a few healthy things, like carrot sticks and hummus and cherry tomatoes. Mostly I eat marshmallows.

"Oh," says Mom, "I meant to tell Pookie I found a camp"—she looks at me and smiles—"thanks to your suggestion."

"Can we afford it?" Joan asks.

"It's free. She'll be a volunteer at an animal therapy camp for kids who are suffering from"—she hesitates, then smiles—"kids with special needs."

I feel my stomach jumping. "Wait. Mom. You're going to let Pookie work with kids? With special needs?"

"Yes, I think it'll be good for her."

I'm not so sure about that. I'm pretty sure it's not going to be good for the kids.

"I hope she'll make some friends," Mom says. "You need to have something to do, too, Julian."

"I have stuff to do. I'm looking for a comet, I'm keeping track of all the Messier Objects that are in the way, just like Mr. Messier, because I can actually see them now, I'm charting where Sirius is in winter and spring so you guys can find me—it—and I'm making friends with Mr. X . . . eventually."

"That's nice, honey, but don't you want us to find friends your own age for you?"

See, that's the problem with Mom. She thinks it's her job to find me friends. Doesn't she think I can do that myself? And I already am. Mr. X. "You don't need to find friends for me, Mom."

"He's fine," Joan agrees. "He's always been good at amusing himself, unlike the Princess of Darkness."

Mom's voice sounds pleading. "But he needs a little friend."

"You mean, like a dog?" I know that's not what she means, but that's what you get for saying I need a *little friend* like I'm four years old. "How about it, Mom? You said you didn't want to have a dog in the city, but we're in the country now."

"Julian, honey, you know your sister's allergic."

"She's allergic to life. And how is she working at an animal camp if she's allergic?"

"It's horses," Mom says, "and it's not the same as living with them. Some of our guests might have allergies, too. I worry that a dog might make people think this place isn't hygienic." She chews her lip. "And everything is in too much of an uproar right now. I can't handle that."

I look to the person who can handle anything. "Joan?"

Joan is sitting hunched over with her head down. "I defer to your mother," she mumbles. Then she pushes away from the table and walks out to the front porch.

What? Joan has an opinion on everything and she'll tell you what it is, too. *I defer to your mother* is not one of them.

I stare at her through the screen door and see Mr. Hale, the lawyer, walking up the stairs as Joan tries to walk down.

He hands her some papers and she squints at them. "Boy, you don't waste any time, do you?"

Mr. Hale shrugs and nods to us through the screen door.

When he sees me he waves. "It was very kind of you to pass on that book and write such a nice letter."

I stand up. "You read my letter?"

"Yes. He wanted me to. You know, he doesn't like kids much, but you're an exception. I hope you keep up this friendship."

Mom stares at me with her mouth open. "Julian, I didn't know you've been—" She runs to the screen door and pushes it open to talk to Mr. Hale. "Is your client safe? Mentally stable? Any criminal record?"

"Mom!"

Mr. Hale shakes his head. "He's harmless, just a sad, broken old soul. It's as if he has nothing left to live for."

"Oh, well, that's fine, then," Mom says.

"Mom!"

"I mean," she says quickly, "it's probably fine for you to be friends."

As soon as Mr. Hale leaves, Pookie comes pounding down the stairs and through the pantry. "What was all that about?"

Mom ignores her and turns to me. "You should've told me you were talking to Mr. X!"

"Why?"

"I've never met him. I need to screen the people you meet. He could be dangerous!"

Pookie rolls her eyes. "He's our next-door neighbor."

"Yes, but we don't *know* him."

"Mom. I was just on his patio. I could yell and you could hear me."

"Really, Mom," Pookie says, "you could expand the kid's bubble just a little."

"I didn't ask you for parenting advice," Mom snaps.

"Maybe you should," I mutter.

Mom doesn't hear me even though I kind of wish she would. I say *Thank you* to Pookie with my eyes and she shrugs *You're welcome* back. She even almost sort of smiles at me even though other people might call it a grimace.

"I'm going to give this Mr. X a call right now"—Mom rummages through the slips of paper on her desk, muttering about his phone number—"and next time he's out, you come get me. Do you understand?"

"Not really, but OK."

"Joan?" Mom says in her *Aren't you with me on this?* voice.

Joan comes in from the porch and sits down at the kitchen table, staring at the papers from the lawyer. And swearing. It starts as a whisper but gets louder.

Mom clears her throat and even though Joan looks over at us, Pookie and I have learned that if your mouth drops open, Joan will stop swearing. If you keep your mouth closed and make your eyes look bored you can really increase your vocabulary.

Joan swears one more string of amazing words and slaps the papers down on the table. "We have twenty days to respond."

I look from Joan to Mom, and back to Joan again. "What does that mean?"

"It's nothing to worry about, Julian," Mom says, punching numbers into her phone. "It's time for you to go to bed."

It's not nearly time for bed. It's not even dark. She's just trying to get rid of me.

I hear her talking to Mr. X on the phone as I leave. "I hope our Julian isn't bothering you. I didn't know he was—" Pause. "Oh, well, thank you. He's a sweet boy. But if he—" Pause. "Ohh-kay, you have a good night, too, bye."

I'm going to have to learn to talk grump-ish like Mr. X, because somehow he stopped Mom from going on and on. That is a real skill.

I hang out by my telescope and watch the sunset while I wait for it to get dark. The sunset is pretty amazing. I like how the oranges and reds get deeper and more intense like orange and red dwarf stars, but I still wish it'd hurry up. When it finally does, I spend a long time looking for a comet.

No luck. I go back to my tree and practically stumble over a rock I haven't seen before. When I pick it up I can tell it's special. I shine my flashlight on it and guess what? You can see the whole universe in this rock. No, really. There are streaks like pulsars and deep dark dense places like black holes and you don't know what's inside, really, except, well, the whole universe. Rocks make up the universe, so if you hold a rock in your hand you're holding the universe.

I climb up to my tree room, lie down, and rest the rock on my chest. It's not heavy but I can feel it. It calms me down but I still can't sleep.

I'm thinking about how we have twenty days to respond to something, even though I'm not sure what it is we're responding to because Mom wouldn't say. Grown-ups always think it's better to hide things from kids but it's not. It makes it worse. You'd think they would've figured that out by now. Don't they know that imagination is more creative than anything real? All I know is that it has to do with Mr. X and I feel kind of bad about it because he's my friend. I also feel bad because being Mr. X's friend is like being a traitor to my family. I'm worried about whose side to be on.

I worry about stuff sometimes. A lot. That's why my therapist gave me a smiley face pillow to throw at the wall. Throwing anything against a wall is violent, and somebody or something is going to get hurt. What was he thinking? I worried about hurting the smiley face guy. And if I didn't throw the pillow against the wall, then I had to worry about what my therapist would think of me for not throwing it against the wall. Sometimes I'd like to throw worry against the wall, but then I'd worry about that, too.

I'm also worrying about how it's all my fault that Pookie is going to be at camp being dramatic with a bunch of special needs kids because she'll probably yell at them and make them all cry. The only thing I can do something about is the kids. I say a kindness meditation for each of them.

FART!

KINDNESS MEDITATION

This is how you say it:

May I be happy*

May I be well

May I be safe from inner and outer danger**

May I be strong

May my life unfold with ease and grace

*You can say meditations for other people, too, you just put their name in where it says ⌊ You should always start with yourself, like putting the airplane oxygen mask on yourself before helping others. That's because you can't help others if you're full of pain, or you can't breathe.

**This means not worrying yourself to death from the inside. And also that no bad guys attack you from the outside.

Since I don't know how many kids Pookie is going to be terrorizing at the camp, I say the kindness meditation thirty times to be sure to cover them all. I also don't know any of their names, so in place of the name I just say *victim*.

14

FLYING TOILETS

I wake up in the middle of the night and see Mr. X's patio light on. I don't see Mr. X so I go look through my telescope. I have eighty-six Messier Objects now. No comet. When I give my eyes a break and look over at Mr. X's patio, he's there, sitting hunched over on the bench, so I go join him.

"Hi, it's me again."

He sighs. "Shouldn't you be asleep?"

"I'm not a very good sleeper."

He grunts. "Me either."

I hold up the rock I found and smile. "This is awesome. Did you know you can see the whole universe in a rock?"

He shrugs. His eyes look so sad my throat is starting to hurt. I don't even mind that he's pinching his nose.

"Mr. X, do you want to find a comet with me?"

"No." His voice is so dull and quiet it's like he's not even alive.

"I could put your name on it and then you could live forever, too."

He doesn't respond.

"You're allowed to put two names on a comet, you know."

He stares straight ahead at where the water would be if our addition wasn't in the way and pinches his nose.

I stand there for a minute in case he changes his mind, but he doesn't. "OK, wish me luck." I start to leave but then turn back. "I'm sorry about our addition. I hate the water, but if I loved lakes, I'd be pretty upset about our house blocking the view."

Slowly he turns his head to look at me and blinks. "Why do you hate the water?"

"You can drown in that stuff."

He shifts a little on his bench. "You can also swim in it."

"If you know how to swim."

"You really don't know how to swim?" He sits up straight and air hisses out of the cushion.

I start rolling and unrolling the straps of my life jacket. "I'm not interested."

"How old are you?"

"Nine-point-six-three."

He stares at me.

"It's approximately nine and two-thirds. Rounding up."

"You should've learned how to swim by now."

"I've had lessons . . . and I—I even have a certificate." I look all around his house and yard and the sky but I can still feel Mr. X staring at the prefrontal cortex of my brain, which I think is where guilt lives.

"Certificate?"

"Uh-huh, yeah." My voice comes out so high and squeaky I have to clear my throat. "From swim class."

"It's a fake," he says.

Asciugamano! How did he know? I must've leaked it out of my brain! "Don't tell, OK?"

"How about you tell me the story?" Mr. X's voice is stronger now.

"Fine," I say because it'd shoot right out of my brain into his, anyway. Whether he knows it or not, he's a uni-sensor just like me. I keep rolling and unrolling a strap from my life jacket.

"After the last class, the teacher was signing certificates which already had our names on them, and putting them on the chair next to her. Some mom distracted her and the teacher just signed them all automatically while she was talking even though she should've skipped mine. And it wasn't a pool we ever went to except for this particular swim class for special needs kids which somehow Mom got me into, and the teacher told her to always wait in the car because her hovering made me more nervous. So when the teacher put my certificate on the chair, I quietly picked it up and walked to the locker room and out the door to the parking lot real smooth like I was Matt Damon in *Ocean's Eleven*, which is an awesome movie, by the way, except that it has *Ocean's* in the title."

Mr. X stares at me for a moment like he's catching up with all the words. "Didn't the teacher call your mother?"

"Well . . . she might've left a message on Mom's cell . . . which I might've accidentally deleted."

Mr. X makes his grumbly noise. "So you still don't know how to swim."

"No. But I'm OK with that."

"Maybe I should have a talk with your mother."

"No! Not Mom. Or even Joan. Please?"

"It's a safety issue. You live right by a lake."

"That's why I'm wearing a life jacket! A conversation about swimming is not necessary. If you want to talk to them about a dog, that's fine, because I'm having a little trouble with that, but not swimming."

He points to the addition, but I know he means the lake. "Do you see that water? Don't you understand how important it is to—"

"Oh, I know, water is very important. Did you know that Matt Damon is trying to get clean water for people around the world? And toilets. Toilets are important, too. There are over seven billion people in this world and two-point-five billion of them don't have toilets, not even a porta potty, so where do they go?"

I don't stop long enough for him to answer even though he tries.

"Wherever they can, which means they pee in the same water where they wash and drink, and they poop in the open or, if they're lucky, in newspaper and then wad it up and throw it as far as possible because who wants to be near their own poop? That's called a flying toilet."

Mr. X tries to speak again but I continue deflecting. I'm pretty expert now.

"I know it seems weird to talk about this stuff, but sometimes you have to address issues that you'd rather avoid in order to make progress. I learned that in therapy, but it hasn't helped me actually solve the world toilet problem yet. It's on my list."

Mr. X holds his palm up to stop me but I keep going.

"I have a plan, though. On November nineteenth, World Toilet Day, I'm going to pass out toilet paper to everyone so I can increase awareness of the situation. It'll be like going trick-or-treating, only in reverse because I'll be giving something not taking it, and it's toilet paper not candy. Pookie says I'm crazy and Mom says I may need to rethink the idea but Joan says she's going to find a Costco and buy me a forty-eight-roll pack."

Once I finally stop barfing all those words, Mr. X starts to talk but I stop him. "So I guess I'll just go to bed now." I give a fake yawn.

"I thought you were looking for comets."

"Suddenly, I'm really sleepy. Good night, Mr. X!"

I wish I hadn't told him that I don't swim. I really, really, really don't want him to mention it to Mom or Joan. Joan will say, *Hey, kiddo! Let's you and me spend some time swimming this summer. It'll be fun!* because she doesn't want to embarrass me but she also doesn't want to let me get away with not learning to swim. Mom will make me read more books about fear and anxiety and how to deal with it. And she'll ask me to please stop worrying. But saying not to worry is like asking the Andromeda Galaxy to stop spiraling toward Earth or asking bullies to stop teasing you. Some things don't stop even when you ask nicely.

And if she doesn't make me read books, she'll practice her movie therapy, which is even worse. She'd probably make me watch *Titanic*.

FART!

THE IMPOSSIBLE

Once Mom tried to help me deal with my fear of drowning by having me watch a movie about a tsunami, *The Impossible*. Even Joan, who's pretty tough, said, "Are you sure this is a good idea?" When people have to ask that, the answer is usually no.

My parallel universe friend Clara is also scared of drowning, so she watched it with me. When the family in the movie started getting swept away in the tsunami, spinning upside down under water with trees and trash hitting them, I couldn't help it, I screamed. Mom jumped and said maybe this was a bad idea and I should stop watching. Clara yelled, *It's a little late for that, isn't it? I can't un-see it now! What were you thinking?* but Mom looked so upset I just said, "I'm OK." And in the end, nobody in the family drowned and they all found each other so even though the movie was called *The Impossible*, I guess sometimes things seem impossible but they're really not. Or it was just a bad movie title and should've been called something like *Horrifying Story of Almost Drowning* or *How to Scare Julian to Death*, because I still had drowning nightmares afterward—and I mean, a LOT.

15

SIRIUS

I kind of avoid Mr. X the next day because I don't want to get into a swimming conversation. Usually he doesn't come out during the day, anyway, mostly at night, which means he could be out soon because we're eating dinner late so it's almost dark. Pookie calls him a vampire or a ghoul. Mom says he's a hermit, which is someone who lives in a cave and doesn't have friends so they're both wrong.

"That explains it," Pookie says at dinner, stabbing the individual kernels of corn on her plate, "he and Julian are exactly the same."

Mom starts to defend me, which will only start an argument, so fortunately Joan says something interesting. "My friend Allison said we could use her time-share on Maui this summer."

"Wait," says Pookie. "*Maui* as in *Hawaii*?" She almost looks happy.

"Impossible," Mom says. "We can't afford it."

Pookie puffs herself up like a puff adder before it strikes. "The time-share is free, right, Joan?"

"It is—"

"But not the airfare," Mom interrupts. She stares at Joan. "You weren't seriously considering this, were you?"

Joan shrugs. "Just for a moment—I mean," she says quickly when Mom's mouth drops open, "only because it might be our last chance for a long time since we don't know what's going to happen here."

Mom shakes her head sternly.

"Jeez, Mom! Do you have to ruin everything?" Pookie stomps up the back stairs.

As much as I hate her shouting, I hate the awkward silence she leaves behind even more. Especially since I can feel the strain between Mom and Joan.

"What's a time-share?" I ask, to get Joan talking, and also because I don't like not knowing things.

Here's what I learn: A time-share is when you can't afford to buy a whole condo in someplace cool like Hawaii so you pay enough to be able to visit it sometimes . . . which gives me an idea so great, I'm even going to risk talking to Mr. X.

I stay up late looking through my telescope, but I never see Mr. X. Just as I finally go to my tree room his patio light comes on and there he is, lying on the bench with his eyes closed. I run over to him.

"Hi, Mr. X, it's me!"

He actually jumps. I guess I woke him up. He squints at me. "What's wrong?"

"Nothing. I have a super massive awesome idea as big as a black hole!"

He makes his rumbling sound. "Can't it wait until morning?"

"I guess it could . . . but now that you're awake it doesn't have to."

He grumbles some more and swings his legs to the ground so he can sit up.

Mr. X opens one eye, which is enough to glare at me, but I sit on the glider chair, anyway. "How would you like a time-share, Mr. X?"

He stares at me for a moment and then at the addition. "I'm not interested in sharing your addition."

"Not that!"

"And I already have a condo in Florida."

"Not the condo kind of time-share, either. The dog kind."

"The dog kind?" He sounds a little bit almost interested, maybe.

"Yeah, it's where you get to enjoy a dog but I do all the work."

"What's the catch?"

"You have to pay for everything. And he has to live at your house."

"Wow, what a deal. Let me think a minute. Gee, I don't even need a minute. The answer is no. Now go to sleep."

"A dog would be good for you."

"You mean, paying for a dog would be good for me."

"You'd get to play with him, too. And go for walks with us. Walking would be good for you. So would playing, actually. And don't worry about him drowning, because I have thirty-four dollars, which is enough to buy him a life jacket that matches mine."

"No dog of mine is wearing a life jacket. If I get a dog, he has to swim."

Suddenly I'm not feeling so good about my idea. "What if he doesn't want to swim?"

"Then I'll throw him in the lake."

I jump to my feet. "What!"

"Dogs are natural swimmers. If you throw them in water they automatically start dog paddling. You've heard that before, right? *Dog* paddling? My dog is going to swim."

"He's not your dog."

"I thought we had a time-share arrangement."

"We do, but—"

"On my time, he swims."

"I'm not sure about this arrangement." I start rolling my life jacket straps.

"You can swim with him, if you want. Or you can watch from the dock."

"I'll watch from the dock."

"Suit yourself."

I keep rolling and unrolling my life jacket straps. I want him to be *my* dog. "His name will be Sirius."

"Serious? Dogs aren't serious."

"No, *Sirius*. The Dog Star. Get it? Dog. And star."

He grunts and shakes his head.

"OK, my second choice for a name is Tobin Maxwell."

He stares at me. "What if it's a girl?"

"Then her name would be Tobin Maxwell."

"Who's Tobin Maxwell? Another scientist?"

"No. I just like the name."

"I don't." He sighs. "Fine. We'll call him—or her—Sirius."

I grin at him. "You'll love Sirius, Mr. X. I know you want a dog."

"I'm too old for a dog, but I'll try to help you get one . . . if you think about swimming."

"What? No. I feel like throwing up whenever I think about swimming."

"That's because you're nervous."

"No, it's because I'm a uni-sensor, which means I'm highly in touch with the universe and it's telling me that swimming is a bad idea."

"So you're going to avoid swimming your whole life? You need to get over this problem."

"It's not a problem. Really. Some people don't drive. They take the bus or a cab or they walk. Some people don't like elevators so they use the stairs instead. They're probably healthier that way. I'm definitely healthier not swimming. Then I won't drown."

"If you learn to swim you won't drown."

I can't believe he just said that. "Are you kidding? People drown all the time!"

"Well, if they get in over their heads and—"

"Over their heads? You can drown in three inches of water! It's happened to people!"

"What people?"

"The dead ones!"

He rolls his eyes.

"No, really! My mom read this book called *Don't Let's Go to the Dogs Tonight.*"

Mr. X scrunches his face up.

"I know, the title is grammatically dubious, but Mom says you have to get past that and into the story, and what happens is this little girl trips and her face lands in a duck pond that's only ankle-deep and guess what? She drowns! That's what!"

He waves his hand. "That's just fiction."

"No! It's a memoir which means the memory of someone's actual life and it actually happened to this girl's actual little sister!"

He throws his head back like he's looking for a particular constellation. "Just think about a dog. And that time-share. Then maybe you'll be interested in swimming."

"If I think about it but decide not to swim, can we still get Sirius?"

He puts his palms on his forehead like Joan does when she has a migraine. "Maybe. But the dog, at least, is going to swim."

I clutch my life jacket as I leave and mutter, "I'm still buying him a life jacket."

"Dream on!" Mr. X calls after me.

FART!

DREAMS

I don't want to dream about drowning, again, so I try to think of other dreams. At school we

always wrote "I Have a Dream" poems in February
in honor of the Reverend Martin Luther King Jr.
Last year mine went on for sixteen pages, and
Mr. Reynolds said he really appreciated my heart
but my hand might appreciate a rest so I stopped.
I could've gone on.

Here are some of the things I wrote that I
still dream about, a lot:

I have a dream that everyone will have a place
to sleep that is not on a sidewalk.

I have a dream that everyone will have food
to eat, even if it's only nutritious food.

I have a dream that kids won't have to work
in sweatshops.

I have a dream that animal abuse will only
happen in history books and when people read it
they'll go, "How could anyone have DONE this?!"

I have a dream that people won't go to
prison when they're bad (just the REALLY bad
ones) but make up for what they did by fixing
whatever they broke and getting to know the
people they hurt and doing nice things for
them.

I have a dream that people who have mental
issues will have nice places to live, therapists to
help take care of them, friends they can make,
and a telescope.*

I have a dream that no one will be mean to
people for being gay or Muslim or an immigrant or
marginally overweight or anything that is just
the way they happen to be.**

 *Because the cosmos can calm people down. It's
magical that way.

 **It's OK to call anyone out on being obnoxious,
no matter who they are. No one gets a free
ride. That's what Joan says.

I have a lot of other dreams, too. Here's one of my new ones:

I have a dream that Pookie will find her dad but still decide
to stay with us.

And I would like to live long enough to see Pookie happy,
but even dreams have their limitations.

16

APOLLO 13

Mom is just getting off the phone when I walk in the kitchen for breakfast. How I know is this: She always says, "Ohh-kay," in a singsongy voice whenever she's about to hang up.

I grab my chance and blurt out, "Do you want to look through my telescope tonight?"

But her eyes are all spacey. "Mr. X is a sweet man, isn't he?" She moves her and Joan's mugs around on the table until they're touching. "I mean, he has his issues, but I think he's mellowing with age."

"Were you just talking to him?"

She nods. "I've been talking to him quite a bit." She gives me a smile that I can tell is fake. "You know, Julian, he really would like to see you be more comfortable in the water. I don't think that swimming class you took was very helpful."

My whole body goes hot and then cold and then hot again. I feel like my face is burning. I give a fake smile, too. "I'm OK with not swimming."

Mom sighs. "I'd feel a lot better if you were a more confident swimmer."

"We're going to be moving away from the lake, anyway."

"We don't know that yet. Things might work out."

I keep deflecting. "Joan says there's no way to compromise on this."

Mom looks at her hands. "I know. I keep hoping for a miracle. I don't want to move. And I know you'd miss Mr. X."

I'm not so sure I'd miss Mr. X since he just ratted on me. I TOLD him not to talk to Mom about swimming!

"I know how you could make him happy. I think he'd be really pleased if he saw you swimming in the lake."

How did she deflect back to swimming again?

She grins. "Don't look so upset. I can watch you. I'll be your cheering section!"

Asciugamano! That's all I need. Mom has been much less helicopter-y than in DC because she's so distracted. Now she's remembering to hover. Thanks a lot, Mr. X! Next thing you know she'll be finding me a doctor.

"By the way," Mom says, "I think I've found the right pediatrician for you. He's—"

I groan. I did it again! Sending thoughts straight to Mom's brain!

"What? Did you want a female doctor? I'll try to find one if you'd prefer. The important thing is for you to be comfortable and happy."

I was comfortable and happy before this whole conversation started.

Pookie yells a really big swear word and comes pounding down the back stairs.

Mom jumps up. "What is it?"

"The toilet overflowed!"

Mom runs for the stairs. "What did you try to flush?"

"It's not my fault! It's this stupid, ancient house! We should've stayed in DC!"

"Come up here and help me!" Mom yells. "And bring a bucket and towels!"

Pookie swears some more, grabs the kitchen towel and a bucket from the pantry, and stomps up the stairs.

Mom's cell phone rings and I automatically run to the kitchen table, grab it, and start to bring it to her. Then I see who's calling. Mr. X. I stop and put her phone down on the kitchen table, harder than necessary, because I'm mad. How could he tattle on me like that? The more I think about it, the madder I get.

I stomp over to Mom's desk, grab a pad of paper and a pencil, and go to my tree room.

Hi, Mr. X,

It's me, Julian. I'm really mad at you. I'm so mad that I'm slowing down my words by writing because if I said them out loud they'd come out too fast and I wouldn't be able to keep the mean things inside. They'd scream at you like they want to right now except I keep stopping and holding my hand up in the air to give it time to think about the consequences. Plus, I have an eraser, just in case.

I thought we were friends. Why did you have to go and talk to Mom about swimming? I TOLD you she would freak. Now she's going to be all helicopter-y again and it's all your fault.

Why would you even DO this? You KNOW I always wear a life jacket. Which Sirius is going to wear, too, because you do NOT just throw a dog into water to make him swim. That's mean and even unconstitutional (Eighth Amendment—cruel and unusual punishment, look it up). I'm not even sure I can trust you with a dog time-share.

Your former friend,
Julian

It's a good thing I'm so mad because my angry legs march me to his front door where I drop my letter without second-guessing myself.

But underneath the mad is sad because not only is Mr. X my former friend, he was also my only friend.

When Joan gets home that night she can tell I'm in a bad mood so she asks what I'd like to do and finally I can ask her to look through my telescope but OF COURSE it's cloudy.

It is really not my day.

So she says, "Let's watch *Apollo 13*," which is one of my favorite movies, even though it's scary, because it has a happy ending and also because it's true.

Apollo 13 was a manned space mission that went wrong. There was an explosion in the main command module that made it lose oxygen and electricity, and the three astronauts had to get in the freezing cold lunar landing module to save all the power in the command module so that maybe, hopefully, it could get them back to Earth.

Then they had a risky maneuver of using the moon's gravity to help fling them back to Earth again while they sat shivering for days wondering if they'd make it or not. It took the NASA engineers and the astronauts working together to solve the problem.

But it wasn't just them. People all over the world were hoping and praying for those three guys, even people who didn't like Americans, because once you're in outer space you're not a nationality anymore, you're just human, and all humans are going to root for you because we're all on the same team.

FART!

THE CONSTELLATION HUMANITY

There isn't really a humanity constellation, but
I like to think it's out there somewhere. That way

we're all together, even when someone dies. They're still part of our universe. They're real. We still remember them and think about them. Memories and thoughts are real. Just because they don't have physical shape doesn't mean they don't exist. Things we can't see and touch are still real, like the air we breathe.

When people die they're not really gone. Not completely, anyway. You can still talk to them. Plus, everything they did changed the course of human events, or at least the course of events in your house. That's true even for people you didn't actually know. Like Abraham Lincoln who wouldn't let our country divide over stupid issues like keeping people enslaved which was a crazy idea to begin with, or Jane Addams who helped immigrants and women and even got the Nobel Peace Prize, or Percy Lavon Julian. They're called inspirations because if they could do something cool, even if it was really hard and took a lot of work and they failed a ton of times but they went back and tried some more until they got it, then we can all do that.

And if we all did that then this world would be a MUCH better place because it wouldn't be just the famous people persevering and contributing, it'd be everyone. That would be a REALLY magical universe.

I wonder if the whole world rooting for me would be enough to get me to learn to swim, without drowning.

Maybe it would.

But I still don't want to risk it.

17

CAFETERIA TRAY
AND THE BVM

Mr. X hasn't shown his face for days, which is pretty smart on his part because I'm still mad at him.

I don't normally like running errands but when Joan asks me to join her I decide to go because it's better than helping Mom with projects or going nowhere on my bike or thinking about Mr. X and how I don't have a friend anymore. At the last minute, Pookie decides to come with us because otherwise Joan will buy the wrong brand of something. So it probably won't be as fun as it could be.

As we're about to pull out of our driveway, Mr. Hale drives by and parks in front of Mr. X's house. Joan hits the brakes and grumbles. "He's always doing that. They're plotting, I guess. Well, we still have two weeks before court, gentlemen, so—"

Pookie makes her orangutan noise. "Do you want me to drive since you're obviously not?"

We peel out of the driveway and end up at the Sav-U-More with the grotto. Joan says I can visit the BVM. Pookie snorts and rolls her eyes, but I run down the path to greet the BVM anyway.

She's still waving so I wave back. She looks a little bit like Mom, only paler.

"Hi, BVM. I like your blue bathrobe. Mom has one just like it."

She doesn't say anything. I wasn't really expecting her to.

"Do you think we become stars after we die? Me too. Do you think we can pick which one we want to be in? I mean, if I really, really, really want to be in Sirius, that's OK, right?"

She doesn't answer. Maybe she's thinking. It looks like she's smiling at me, so I'm uni-sensing yes.

But when I start complaining about Mr. X and what a rat he is she stops smiling and says I have to go. I guess she doesn't like mean thoughts. "So-rry," I mutter, but she says I have to go because I need to take care of my sister.

Why does she say that?

I don't know, but it makes me nervous and I run up the path as fast as I can.

I head for the store, but what I see beyond the store stops me. It's Pookie, bending over a red Camaro, and a boy looking at her butt.

What's weird is that even though Pookie says sporty cars are stupid, she's now leaning on it, staring at the cool stripes on the side.

The guy is grinning and also snuffing up, wiping his nose with the back of his hand, which would normally gross Pookie out but she doesn't even seem to notice.

He's staring at her shorts. I never got why Mom had such a fit about writing on the backs of shorts. Until now. It's taking him forever to read one word. I want to shout, "Sound it out! It's not that hard! East-ern!"

When she finally turns around and looks up at him, he doesn't actually look at her. Well, he doesn't look at her face, more like her chest. I'm worried because Pookie seems to be enjoying it. She's smiling so much her mouth is open and his head is over hers so that if a booger fell out of his nose it would land right in her mouth. Gross!

I walk up next to her but she doesn't even notice.

"Nice wheels," Pookie says.

"Thanks. You drive?"

"Don't have my license—yet. My parents are SO overprotective." She rolls her eyes.

That may be true, but that's not why she doesn't have a license. She's only 14.2.

"Well, if you ever need a ride, I can take you. I live right there." His head jerks to the right but his eyes never leave Pookie's chest.

I step between them. "That's OK, we have a Subaru Outback and it has EyeSight and all kinds of safety features so—"

"Who are you?"

Pookie makes a low, warning orangutan sound.

"I'm her brother, Julian. Who are you?"

"*Julie*-in?" He smirks like that's a funny name, which makes me mad. Percy Lavon Julian is no one to make fun of!

"What's your name?" I ask.

"Trey," he says.

"Tray? Like in a cafeteria?"

"Shut up!" Pookie hisses.

"At least I'm named after someone famous, Percy Lavon Julian—"

"I said, shut up!" Pookie hisses, louder.

"Joan wants you," I say, although I don't know why that came out of my mouth.

She starts to answer but Joan's yell interrupts her. "Pookie!"

"I'm busy!"

Joan narrows her eyes, tilts her head, and puts her hands on her hips. "I need to ask you something."

Pookie turns away and looks at Trey's car.

"Fine," Joan says, "I'll buy the generic."

Pookie makes her full-blown orangutan noise and hurries over to Joan while Trey keeps reading EAST-ERN on her butt.

I step in front of him to block his view. "See that lady my sister's talking to?"

"What of it?"

"That's Joan. She was a Merchant Marine."

He doesn't look impressed.

"She could arm wrestle anyone at the fire station. And usually win."

He shrugs.

"She can bench-press three hundred pounds."

He's starting to look a little impressed.

"If you touch my sister, Joan will kick you in the nuts." I'm not sure Joan would actually do that, but I'm not sure she wouldn't, either.

Pookie starts walking back to Trey, smiling at him.

He hurries to get inside his Camaro, revs the engine, and drives away.

Pookie glares at me. "What did you say to him?"

"Nothing."

She grabs my arm.

"I just told him who Joan was."

"Thanks for ruining any chance I had of having a friend!" She lets go of me and pushes me away.

"WE used to be friends," I remind her.

"Right, *used to be*. Past tense! I am SO done with you, Julian."

It's the first time she's called me Julian in forever. I thought I didn't like it when she called me squirt or freak or stupid, but at least she was being my sister. Now she's talking to me like I'm a stranger, or in a different universe.

"Kids," Joan calls, "come get these bags in the car."

Joan fills up the tank and asks, "Who was that boy?"

"Trey," Pookie mutters.

"Ray?" Joan says.

"TRAY," I tell her, "like in a cafeteria."

"Treeeeey," Pookie says, rolling her *r*'s—or maybe she's gritting her teeth.

"Ah," says Joan, "Treeeey, like in a *French* cafeteria."

Pookie storms to the front passenger seat of the Outback and slams the door while Joan winks at me.

I try to smile but it doesn't work.

As we pull out of the Sav-U-More, Joan says, "Hey, you kids want to stop for ice cream?"

"No, thank you!" Pookie spits out.

I shake my head.

"Boy, you two are a barrel of fun."

Which reminds me of the Barrel of Monkeys game Pookie and I used to play. It was just a bunch of plastic monkeys you could hook together by their arms and tails, but we'd dangle them from our ears or put them places to surprise Mom and Joan like inside the fridge or shower, or hang them from the car's rearview mirror.

I look at Pookie and wonder if she's remembering that, but she's staring out the window so I can't even see her face.

After unloading the car I escape to my tree room, but before I climb up I stop because there's a puffy envelope on the ground. From Mr. X.

When I open it, two things fall out:

1. A pair of swim goggles, which I let stay on the ground
2. A metal tag shaped like a fire hydrant with SIRIUS etched onto it that makes me smile

It's weird how you can have the best and the worst gift in the same package.

There isn't a note, but I know it has to be from Mr. X. It means we're getting Sirius. But only if I swim.

FART!

M_{51}

I think it's pretty magical that the very next Messier object I record is M_{51} in the constellation Canes Venatici, which means *hunting DOGS*. The part that makes me queasy is that M_{51} is the WHIRLPOOL Galaxy. I hope there's no connection.

18

ONE SMALL STEP

When I go inside the next morning, Joan is swearing and banging around upstairs, Mom is muttering and banging around in the kitchen, and Pookie is moving her stuff into the pantry. She's stacking up mac and cheese boxes to make room for her **DAD** picture frame that doesn't have a picture inside, just a piece of paper that says ROOM ESSENTIALS 8 X 10.

"What's going on?"

Pookie stops long enough to make a face at me, and not a happy one. "Joan is"—she rolls her eyes—"fixing the toilet. So I'm moving down here while she works on it."

"Oh. She might fix it," I say.

"Right, when we land on Mars."

"Actually, that's already happened. We landed Viking probes on Mars"—Pookie is glaring at me so hard I finish with—"but I know what you mean."

Occasionally Joan can fix things just fine, but most of the time she spends days taking something apart, another day swearing at it, and then we call a professional. Mom ends up clearing away Joan's mess and saying something like, "Well, at least you gave it a try," except it comes out sounding more like, "Well, that was a complete waste of time," and then Joan gets mad and goes out for a walk, which she normally never does so at least it's good for her health.

I shrug. "Well, the weather's nice now."

Pookie snorts. "Then Joan can have a nice walk."

I find the pliers and sit down at the kitchen table to put Sirius's tag on my safety bracelet.

That's when Mom finally notices me. "What's your new charm?"

"It's not a charm. It's a tag. For Sirius."

Mom scrunches up her face because she doesn't understand.

"It's the name of my dog," I explain, "when we get one."

"What!" Pookie yells from the pantry. "Doesn't anyone care what I think? The world stops spinning if Julian even sneezes but if I'm allergic to dogs it's OK because we have to do whatever Julian wants?"

"I never said—" Mom begins but Pookie interrupts her.

"You make me go to a stupid camp to take care of sick kids—like I don't do that all the time at home! Then—"

Mom starts to interrupt but it doesn't work.

"—you take away my room—"

"It's temporary," Mom snaps, "and I thought you didn't like your room."

"It's a stupid room but it was mine! So I'm sleeping in a pantry? My dad would at least give me a bedroom! And now we're getting a dog even though I'm allergic! Am I invisible here?"

Mom starts to answer but stops suddenly. I think she's looking at the dog tag again so I hold up my arm for her to see it, and to deflect her from arguing with Pookie. She grabs my wrist but looks farther up my arm.

"What's that?"

I shrug. "A bug bite, I guess."

"Aren't you using the mosquito net?"

"Yes." That's mostly true.

She stares closer at the bump. "How could this have happened?"

Pookie walks into the kitchen, holding out her arms, which are covered in bites. "It's called Deadwater, Maine."

Mom doesn't even look at Pookie. I wish she would. It's making me nervous the way she's staring at my one bite.

"Antibiotics," she breathes, finally dropping my arm and running to the kitchen cabinet. She starts opening cabinet doors frantically and slamming them shut. She swears under her breath and runs past us through the pantry, up the back stairs, yelling for Joan.

Pookie rolls her eyes.

I wonder if I'm going to die. I thought I had more time. My family doesn't even know how to find Sirius yet!

Joan has antibiotics in her kit, but Mom is practically crying in the two minutes it takes for Joan to find them. Mom watches me swallow one.

"It's going to be OK," Mom says, still breathless. "It's going to be OK."

I'm not sure if she's saying it to herself as a mantra, or to me. Either way, it makes my heart jump around in my chest, which is definitely not good for it.

When Mom and Joan start arguing, I feel sick. Mom wants Joan to give me a shot. Joan says that's only for emergencies.

"It's always an emergency when it comes to Julian," Pookie says, to no one in particular.

Mom's and Joan's words swirl around some more. Mom wants to get me to a hospital, stat.

Joan says she's overreacting.

"Ya think?" Pookie says. "That's a first!"

When Joan tells her to stop and Pookie says something rude, although to be fair it's an expression she learned from Joan, both Mom and Joan start yelling at Pookie, which gives me time to slip outside.

But I can't help thinking that Pookie's lip quivered a bit when they were yelling at her even though she kept unpacking her books and sticking them around the **DAD** picture frame. And how come, if Pookie's arms are covered in bites, they aren't worried about her even a teeny bit?

Although Pookie is *difficult*, which is the nice way of saying a galactic pain in the butt, she's still my sister. She saved my life. A lot. When I was five, I was trying to fly so I jumped off the roof of the garage even though Pookie yelled at me to stop. She ran and caught me just in time so she ended up with a concussion and broken arm instead of me. When I was seven, I almost fell out of a moving car that was too old to have safety features and the door I was leaning against opened and I saw the road headfirst but just before I hit, I felt myself sucked back into the car and it was Pookie pulling me inside. And last year some kids tried to beat me dead because I'm a freak and Pookie screamed in like Wonder Woman, or maybe more like a Dementor, and scared them all so much they ran away and had to wait until the next day to apologize.

It makes my throat hurt just thinking about it. That's the sister I miss. Joan says she'll be back again when she becomes more like herself. But if we keep treating her like she's not herself, when will that happen?

From my tree room I hear all three of them arguing and Joan calling Pookie the Princess of Darkness again, which makes me scrunch up my face and close my eyes.

Mom says she should've taken me to the pediatrician long ago and Joan says I was just there a few weeks ago and I was fine. Mom calls the pharmacy and puts the recording on speaker. I know that recording by heart. I don't even have to go to the doctor for antibiotics anymore. Mom just calls the pharmacy and they say, "Oh, it's for that Julian kid? Antibiotics is his major food group!"

I try to shut out the yelling by meditating, but all I see is Mom clutching her plastic Target bag of stuff, Joan with the sack of bottles rattling on her back, and Pookie sinking under the weight of her cauldron.

Finally, I hear, "Knock-knock" from the bottom of my tree.

I look down. "Oh, hi, Joan."

"Hi, kiddo. Just letting you know that I've talked your mother out of whisking you off to the hospital."

"Thanks."

"But you're supposed to tell us if you feel sick or weak or dizzy or can't breathe or—well, you know the drill."

I nod. "Hey, Joan?"

"Yup?"

I go down to her because I don't really want anyone else to hear what I have to say. I've been thinking about it for at least an hour, which is how long it has taken for Joan to calm Mom down.

"What is it, kiddo?"

I almost cringe. "Do you want to go sit on the patio?"

"That's not our patio."

"Mr. X doesn't mind."

She stares at the patio for a moment and grimaces. "Fine."

I sit on my regular glider chair and she sits on the edge of the bench where Mr. X usually sits, but she keeps looking at it like she thinks there's bird poop all over it.

I roll and unroll my life jacket straps and Joan says, "What's up, kiddo?" which makes me cringe again and I just blurt out, "Could you maybe please sometimes call Pookie kiddo instead of the Princess of Darkness because, I mean, I know she acts that way all the time but—"

"But it's name calling," Joan says, "and probably makes her behave even worse." She lets out a swear word.

"Are you mad at me?" I ask her.

"No. I'm mad at myself. And embarrassed. I just got schooled in parenting by a nine-year-old."

"You get an A-plus in all the other parenting stuff, though."

"Thanks, kidd—" but she stops herself.

"It's OK, you can still call me kiddo, too."

"All right," she says, rubbing her hands together, "let's put this new plan into action!"

I breathe a big sigh and follow Joan inside. I like how Joan doesn't make a big deal out of stuff. Mom would look at me with teary eyes and go all gushy about how sweet and sensitive I am, which always makes me want to blow a really big fart noise on my arm to prove I'm just a regular kid.

I also like how when Joan says she'll do something, she does. And right away, too. "Special lunch!" she yells as she pulls food out of the fridge, telling everyone to come in the kitchen.

Pookie stares at the sandwich stuff. "This is the special lunch? I'm not eating that!" She turns and stalks back to her pantry.

"It's build your own sandwich day! Then we'll go out for ice cream. How does that sound, kiddo?"

Pookie doesn't answer.

"She's talking to you," I tell Pookie.

She turns on me but then sees Joan smiling at her. "I thought you were talking to him," she says in her sneer-y voice. "He's the kiddo."

"You're my kiddo, too," Joan says, still smiling, and her eyes have this way of holding you in a tractor beam and it makes you feel safe.

"That is so stupid," Pookie says and rolls her eyes.

But guess what? She walks over to the counter and even though she says, "This is the wrong mayo" and, "I hate this kind of bread" and, "Ew! There's gristle in this ham," she builds her own sandwich.

Mom raises her eyebrows. Joan winks at me and we all pass a smile around behind the new kiddo's back.

I feel like the astronaut Neil Armstrong: That's one small step for Pookie, one giant leap for our family. I'd like to suggest a telescope party but I don't want to push my luck. I think I just have to wait until I uni-sense the right time.

FART!

THE FIRST PERSON ON THE MOON

Actually, what Neil Armstrong said was this: That's one small step for a man, one giant leap for mankind. He was the first guy on the moon and he knew everyone would be listening to him because no one on Earth had ever been to the moon before so he spent a long time thinking of something special to say. I think he did a pretty good job. He's saying you start out small but once you start you can do great things. It applies to space exploration and even to life.

19

GIFTED

That night, when I'm heading back from my telescope—no comet—Mr. X is on his patio, but I walk right past him without saying a word because I'm still mad that he ratted on me about swimming. The totally awesome dog tag he gave me is cancelled out by the totally not awesome swim goggles.

He makes his rumbling sound.

"I'm not talking to you right now," I say, even though, technically, I just did.

I can feel Mr. X stand up. "I know I can be annoying sometimes but it's for a good cause."

I stop. I hate when my own words are used against me. It makes me feel like I have to listen because if I thought those words were important enough to say then it's kind of hypocritical of me to ignore them.

I sigh and turn around. "OK, I'll talk to you, and I know you're trying to be helpful but I'm NOT ready to talk about swimming."

He bows his head and holds a hand up, palm out. "Truce. We'll call a moratorium on swimming talk for the moment."

I go sit on my usual glider chair and he sits on his bench.

He claps his hands together slowly and softly. "Sooo, what do you want to talk about?"

"Dogs. But not the *if you swim we'll get a dog* kind of dog, just dogs in general."

"OK," he says, "you first."

"We need a dog because dogs are natural love sponges. They soak up love and when you hug them, love squeezes back out again."

He nods and swallows.

"When a dog kisses you it means *thank you* and *please* at the same time."

He nods again.

"There's magic inside a dog. They have antiseptic properties in their saliva and that's why they lick their wounds. That's not why they lick their butts. Who knows why they do that?"

His mouth goes into a line, which is sort of like a smile, at least for Mr. X. I can uni-sense that he's feeling warm and fuzzy and gushy so I say, "Can you tell me about Taurus, the dog in all the pictures?"

So he tells me lots of Taurus stories. They're everything I ever imagined about having a dog for a friend. Even the naughty stuff.

Mr. X squints at the patio door and points to one of the dog sketches on the wall. "See that smirk? I drew that one right after he chewed up something or other."

"You drew that? Did you draw all of them?"

"Yeah." He shrugs like it's no big deal.

"You're an artist!"

He snorts. "Nah, I just draw what I know. I knew that dog. Real well." He starts to talk about when Taurus died but stops. And pinches his nose. He looks all sad again.

I try to deflect. "Dogs are like life. They're an amalgamation of good and fun and sweet and even a little bit sad but they're worth it."

"Amalgamation?"

"It's a fancy word that means Chex Mix."

"Amalgamation is quite a word for a kid. English teachers must love you."

"Mostly. Sometimes I'm not very good with assignments. Like when they ask, *Why did the author say this?* There could be a million reasons why. I can think of lots. You can narrow it down, but nobody can say exactly why the author said something except the author. And sometimes I bet they don't even know. I don't always know why I say something."

"I changed my mind. Teachers must find you annoying."

"No, most teachers are OK with thinking. They believe in asking questions. School systems don't like it, though. They want one answer bubble to fill in on the electronic score sheet and that's it. Done. But the universe is not that simple. Maybe some people think it is, but I don't. My answers don't fit inside a bubble."

"Your mother says you're gifted. Doesn't that mean you have all the answers?"

"No. I have a lot of questions. I hardly have any answers."

"Then why do they call you gifted if you're not that smart?"

"Because it's not that kind of gifted. It's emotionally gifted. That means I think about things a lot and care about people's feelings and know what they're thinking and know what they're going to say or do and it takes me a long time to make a decision because I think about the effects of every possible thing I say and do.

"Like on the playground when kids say, *Do you want to play tag?* they expect you to answer in less time than they give you on *Jeopardy!*, which is five seconds, I counted. It's like they don't even think. I have to feel my body and how other people are feeling. And I have to check the weather because if I play tag some people will get mad if I stop to look at the clouds. Or if it's a good day for swinging I might want to do that but if the swings are crowded I might as well play tag. Which kids are playing tag is important, too, because if it's rough kids you risk getting knocked down. And if it's the popular kids, which it usually isn't because why would they ask me, but if it is, who else is getting left out? Will they be sad? Will they be mad at me because I'm a traitor to the not popular kids? So it takes me a long time to answer and then kids think I'm stuck up or stupid, but actually *Do you want to play tag?* is a very hard question."

Mr. X stares at me for a long time.

I shrug. "It's the way my brain works. It's not fun. At all. It just is."

He pinches his nose. "In my day they called that neurotic."

"I've heard that before. I guess they changed the name."

"Guess so. Gifted, huh?"

I nod. "Sometimes I'd like to regift it and get another gift instead."

"Like what?"

"A comet."

"That's a pretty tall order."

"It can happen! And it will."

"Yeah, OK. What else?"

"I want my family to look through my telescope and find the Dog Star and appreciate the magic of the universe."

"Boy, you really aim high, kid, don't you? What else?"

I sigh. "A dog."

"That one's doable."

"Not really."

"What would you say if I could get you a dog—and your family to accept it?"

"I would say you're a magician. But the good kind who makes real magic happen, not fake magic."

"It wouldn't take magic."

"Have you talked to my mom about this? Because she'll say no."

"I'll take care of it."

"Will you take care of Joan?"

He nods. "I have a plan. You hold up your end of the bargain, which is to think about swimming."

So I do hold up my end of the bargain.

FART!

FEMTOSECONDS AND ASTRONOMICAL UNITS

A femtosecond is one-quadrillionth of a second. That's one-millionth of one-billionth of a second. It's really small. That's how long I think about swimming.

An astronomical unit (AU) is the distance between Earth and the sun: ninety-three million miles. It changes a bit depending on where Earth is in its orbit around the sun, but basically it's still really, really, really far. That's how far away I'd like to be from the stupid lake.

When I get to my tree I find another rock. It looks like it's from a meteor, straight from outer space. For a second I wonder if it might be Mr. X who's leaving me rocks. I wave over at him and yell, "This rock is awesome!"

He kind of shrugs and waves back.

OK, maybe it's not him.

I take my new rock to bed with me. Now I have two magical* rocks on my chest.

*They're magical because I don't have the drowning nightmare at all!

20

SURVIVAL

Even though Mr. X said he'd give me some time to think about swimming, he only gives me three days and he's pacing on his patio, arguing with me.

"You're not being rational!"

"Mr. Anxiety isn't known for being rational," I explain.

He stops pacing and stares at me. "What?"

I let out a big sigh as I unroll my life jacket strap. "It's not ME, it's Mr. Anxiety talking."

"Well, I don't want to talk to Mr. Anxiety! I want to talk to Julian!"

"I'm sorry, he's not available right now."

Mr. X lets his breath out fast and loud. "So you're not going to talk to me?"

I keep rolling and unrolling the straps of my life jacket. "I might be talking to you. We might be talking in a parallel universe at this very moment. You never know."

He says some of Joan's swear words.

"Mom wouldn't like to hear you swearing like that."

"Mom doesn't need to know, then, does she?"

"Mom didn't need to know about swimming but you told her anyway."

"Oh, for—" He stops himself and makes his grumbly sound instead.

I guess I'm still kind of mad at him about the whole swimming issue so I add, "And anyway, that was a dumb thing to send Joan."

"A local Maine dinner basket is *dumb*?"

"The only kind of fish Joan likes is Filet-O at McDonald's."

"That wasn't fish! That was an expensive lobster!"

"Well, she doesn't like it. Or wine."

"Fine! What does she like? Flowers?"

"Are you kidding? She says it's the gift that keeps on giving chores. First you have to find a vase, then you have to mix up that packet of solution so the flowers don't die right away, then you have to pick up the petals that keep dropping, then—"

"OK, OK, I get the idea. How about chocolate?"

I nod.

"What kind?"

"Pretty much any kind as long as it's chocolate."

What I don't know is why Mr. X is sending Joan stuff. Doesn't he know she's already married?

"Joan was a Merchant Marine," I blurt out. I'm not trying to scare him, exactly. Just make him aware.

It gets his attention. "Really? There aren't that many women in the Merchant Marines."

"Well, she was. She's really strong."

He nods. "I like strong women."

I start rolling and unrolling my life jacket straps double time.

Mr. X squints at me. "Is something wrong? Other than your usual nervousness?"

"You know she's married to my mom, right?"

He grumbles. "No. I did not know that."

"So she's not available."

"Excuse me?"

"You can't date her."

"I don't want to date her! First of all, I'm probably forty years older than she is!"

"Mom says old men are always making fools of themselves going after younger women."

He grunts. "I've made a fool of myself in lots of ways, but that's not one of them."

"Then how come you're being so nice to Joan?"

"I have my reasons."

"Like what?"

"You want a dog, don't you?" he snaps.

I nod and stop rolling my life jacket straps. "How come Joan isn't nice back to you?"

"She has her reasons."

"What are they?"

"No idea."

Mr. X looks so sad I try to think of something nice to say. "Mom liked the Maine dinner basket. A lot."

"She told me. She didn't mention Joan hated it, though."

"Of course not, that would be rude. Then she'd probably have to add a manners book to the Target bag she hauls around, and that thing is already pretty heavy."

"What Target bag?"

"Oh. Never mind. It's too long to explain."

He looks almost relieved. "I'll take care of the chocolates and tomorrow we start swimming lessons."

"Tomorrow?" I clutch my life jacket. "I was thinking next week."

"Tomorrow. And ditch the life jacket."

I can't help it. I clutch my life jacket even harder. "Why?"

Mr. X lets out a long breath. "It's a *swimming* lesson. What would you need a life jacket for?"

"I thought lesson one would be an overview."

"An overview?"

"An overview is the talking part. We can do that right here."

"It's swimming. What's there to talk about? You get in the water!"

"Aren't you going to give me any instruction?"

"Yeah, when you get in the water!"

"But what about pre-learning?"

"You learn by doing! In the water!"

"I don't function as well that way. I might freeze up and drown."

Mr. X bugs his eyes out at me.

"I'm just trying to save you from being a complete failure as a teacher. And the embarrassment of having to bring my cold, limp body to my family."

After some swearing, he calms down a bit and we come up with a compromise:

Lesson one will be on the dock but it is ONLY talking and I can wear my life jacket. I guess Mr. X will do OK once he figures out "what the Sam Hill pre-learning is." Me I'm not so sure about.

FART!

SURVIVAL

Sometimes people will surprise you.

People get crushed in buildings after an earthquake or stuck in the snow after a plane crash or survive without water longer than anyone thought was humanly possible. One guy even cut his own arm off so the rest of him could live. There are millions of people like that every day. It could be small things like finding food or not getting beaten up or convincing your mom that marshmallows for dinner every once in a while is OK (that is a HUGE accomplishment, by the way).

Some people call it the human spirit. Others call it the will to survive. I call it magic. Unfortunately for me, I don't think I have that kind of magic when it comes to swimming.

I'm worrying so much about swimming I can't get to sleep. I even forget about my magic rocks. I try counting stars but it's really stressful because you can see so many stars in the night sky here that it's easy to miss one, or think you missed one, so I have to keep going back and starting over because I don't want to ignore a single star. If I do, the people in that star will feel forgotten and lonely. I can't let that happen. It's too sad.

I do finally get to sleep because I keep waking up from my drowning nightmare. It's REALLY exhausting drowning over and over and over.

Thanks a lot, Mr. X.

21

SWIMMING

I can tell it's hot because I can feel the sun on my head and the dock is warm on the soles of my feet but in between my head and feet I'm shivering.

Mr. X sighs. "Why don't you take off the life jacket now?"

"It's too cold."

"It's one of the warmest days we've had. If it got any hotter I'd be dead from heatstroke."

I roll and unroll the straps of my life jacket. "I'm good, thanks."

Actually, I'm not good. I feel dizzy. It's not the swimming so much that scares me—I can swing my arms and kick my legs. My arms are strong from stationary rowing and my legs are strong from stationary biking. It's the getting in the water part that scares me. Like right now, I feel as if that hard plastic mask is covering my face and I can't breathe and the whole world is going fuzzy and it sounds gurgle-y and my life is about to be over. THAT'S what's going to happen if I get in this super massive black hole of water. I'll get sucked in and never come back. I'm just not ready for that. I'd like to at least have a dog before I go up to the Dog Star forever.

I look away and see Mom standing outside the kitchen door on her phone, or pretending to be on her phone. I think she's really watching me. I wish she wouldn't. It just makes me more nervous.

Also, I'm missing some pre-learning. I know because I hear Mr. X say, "Are you even listening?"

When I look up to answer him I get dizzy, stumble backward, and almost fall into the water.

"Asciugamano!" I yell and run off the dock to dry land.

"What do you need a towel for?" Mr. X says. "You're not even wet."

That snaps me out of my dizziness and I stop. "Wait. How do you know Italian?"

"My family's Italian. What's your excuse?"

"I like Italian because I want to go to Italy. And it's the language of love."

"Any language is the language of love if you use the right words."

We both stare at each other because that's not a very Mr. X–like thing to say.

He makes his grumbly sound. "Why don't you learn Spanish? It's more useful."

"OK." I start walking to the house.

"Hey! Where are you going?"

"To learn Spanish."

"I didn't mean right now! We barely started our lesson."

"That's enough for today. I don't need to be an overachiever."

"You haven't achieved anything yet!"

I squint my eyes at him because that was a mean thing to say. "I think I liked you better when you stayed on your patio."

"Look," he says, pointing at the dock, "I'm only here because of you."

Maybe Pookie's right. Maybe I should work harder at keeping my thoughts inside my own mutant brain and everyone's life would be easier.

I go to the house because I'm worried that if I go to my tree room Mr. X will follow me and try to get me to go swimming again. Mom runs into the kitchen ahead of me like she really wasn't watching me all along even though she was.

Inside, everyone is arguing, as usual. It's definitely not the language of love. Pookie is extra angry now because Mom and Joan decided that even though the plumber fixed the toilet (and Mom got annoyed and Joan took her walk), Pookie should sleep on a cot in the pantry so they can rent out the Jack and Jills. Maybe it's a test to see if only having the Jack and Jills will bring in enough money without using the addition. I don't know. I just know that Pookie is madder than usual.

"And anyway," Pookie is shouting from the pantry, "I'm not going back to that camp ever again!"

"Maybe that little girl will be OK," Joan says. "Maybe she'll be back next week."

"No, she won't! That's the whole point! It's a camp for sick kids who aren't going to get better, so she's not coming back! She's—"

"Pookie!" Mom yells, looking at me.

Pookie slams a cabinet door.

"Hey!" Joan says. "Stop slamming the—"

"I don't like it any more than you do," Pookie says, "but I don't have a bedroom door, remember?" And she slams the cabinet door again. Twice.

Joan heads for the pantry and Mom grabs her arm and they start whisper-arguing, which sounds like hissing. You can't hear the words but they feel like, "I'm so exasperated with you!" and, "Well, I'm exasperated with you, too!"

It gets my stomach acid rising like a tsunami every time one of them says, "Why can't you just—" and then you can't hear the words after that, and the other one says, "BECAUSE—" and then her voice drops to a whisper.

I decide I have to go visit Mr. X even if he tries to get me to go swimming again. He's sitting on his bench, so I sit down on the glider.

"You back for a lesson?"

I shake my head. "I have hormone overload."

"Aren't you a little young to be having hormone issues?"

"Not mine." I look at our house. "Theirs. It's estrogen poisoning."

Mr. X pinches his nose and looks around like he doesn't know what to say.

"Have you ever tried living with three women?" I ask him.

"No."

"I didn't think so."

Right then, Mom's voice rises even louder than the others. Her anxiety can make her do that sometimes.

"Your mom's a little . . . tightly wound, isn't she."

"You should've seen her when she was a doctor. Especially when her patients died."

"How many of her patients died?"

"Just some. She's really a good doctor."

"Right. Remind me never to make an appointment with your mother."

I feel a bubbly laugh come out of my stomach and through my mouth.

"What's so funny?"

"She's an ob-gyn! Do you know what kind of doctor that is?"

"Yeah, yeah." He waves his hand at me and turns away like I farted. "Titties and hoo-hah."

"What? Actually, the correct terminology is—"

"I don't want to hear it. A kid shouldn't mention female body parts."

"Then what am I supposed to say? Titties and hoo-hah?"

"Sounds funny when a kid says it."

"It sounds even funnier when a grown-up person says it."

He grunts. "Sometimes I don't act very grown-up."

"That's OK. Me either."

He almost smiles. "What are you going to be when you grow up?"

I shrug. "I never think about that."

"Every kid thinks about what they want to be when they grow up. How about astronaut?"

I shake my head. "Astrophysicist. Like Neil deGrasse Tyson." I don't tell him I'll probably never get that old.

Mom's voice is still scream-y but now it's calling my name.

"I'm right here!"

"Well, come in this minute! It's time to eat! And then we're having a family meeting."

I sigh. *"Asciugamano."*

"Good luck, kid," Mr. X says.

Turns out the family meeting is about renting out the Jack and Jill rooms, which I'd already guessed and really doesn't involve me since I have a tree room so I ignore it and think about the universe. Pookie is having a hard time ignoring it and she's making the meeting longer with her yelling.

When Mom and Joan argue with each other for a moment I whisper to Pookie, as nicely as I can so she won't get mad, "Just go to a parallel universe until it's over."

She narrows her eyes at me and opens her mouth to yell.

"It really works," I say, nodding my head fast. "Mom and Joan won't be there."

She closes her mouth and even almost smiles. At least she looks happier for the rest of the meeting. And she's quiet.

After dinner, Mr. X isn't around so I go look through my telescope. Still no comet.

When I get to my tree room there's *another* rock! I wonder again if it's possible, somehow, that Mr. X is putting them here for me. And if it is, does he want it to be like a Secret Santa thing where I'm not supposed to know it's him? I take it up to my room and remember to put all three rocks on my chest before I close my eyes. At least I won't have the drowning nightmare now.

I think about what Mr. X said, and he's right. Any language can be the language of love. For instance, when he said, *Good luck, kid* to me tonight that was as good as a grandfather saying, *I love you*. Really. That's what Westley means in *The Princess Bride* when he says, *As you wish*. Sometimes it's hard for people to say, *I love you* so they have to use other words.

Mr. X is also right that it'd be smart to learn Spanish because I can use it more. Plus, I already know some Spanish:

Hola! (Hello!)

Adiós! (Goodbye!)

Si desea continuar en español, elija número dos.

That's the pharmacy recording, which basically means, *If you want to continue in Spanish, press two*. I hear it on speakerphone when Mom orders my antibiotics, which is like every other week because all I have to do is cough or sneeze and she panics.

Sometimes I hear that lady's voice in my sleep . . . *Si desea continuar en español, elija número dos.*

FART!

ASTRONAUTS

I could never be an astronaut. For one thing, they have to learn to scuba dive. Under. Water. I know! I probably wouldn't pass the physical, either, because I have heart palpitations just thinking about training underwater.

Plus, there's the motion sickness. They make you ride on a plane called the Vomit Comet. No, really. If it makes regular people puke, just think what it would do to me! Maybe they have super strong motion sickness medicine but still, the other stuff you can't fix.

Besides, I'll be in outer space soon enough. I don't need to be an astronaut.

22

WIMP

Mr. X will not give up on swimming. He says we have to have lessons every single day. Which includes getting wet.

I make a sneer-y Pookie face at him as I hold on to one of the posts on the dock and lower my left foot close to the water.

"Come on, kid," he mutters.

I actually dip my entire big toe in the water, but it's so cold I run screaming off the dock to dry land. I hear Mr. X swearing behind me.

Pookie is in a lawn chair in the front of the house. Even though she's wearing sunglasses I know she's rolling her eyes at me. "Jeez, squirt, you're such a wimp!"

"You don't have to watch me," I tell her.

"Yes, I do. Mom is making me."

"But I don't need you, I have—"

"I know. But it's MOM, right? I don't like it any more than you do."

"So-rry," I say, all sarcastic, "that I'm wasting your precious time."

"It's not that, dork—well, it's that—but also it's not letting you step out of the house without one of us having to watch you. How does she ever expect you to be normal if we treat you like a freak? And what's the big deal with swimming, anyway?"

"I don't want to swim because I'll die."

"That's stupid."

"People die all the time. Like that girl at therapy camp," I say, because now I know why Pookie's not going back. She's mad that one of the kids died.

"Shut up about her!" Pookie yells, but I can feel the hurt screaming in her voice.

"She's still here, Pookie. She's up in the stars and you can talk to her. The universe is incredible."

"The word *incredible* means *not credible* which means *not believable*."

"But that's just it, it's incredible but it happens anyway! It's magic! Actually, it's science. Like Neil deGrasse Tyson says, the good thing about science is that it's true whether or not you believe in it."

"To be honest, I don't care so just shut up."

"To be completely honest," I say back to her, "I wish you were still at therapy camp."

Pookie's lips start wobbling and now I really, really wish I hadn't said that about therapy camp because that was mean. "You're either honest or not, dork. There's no such thing as *completely* honest."

Actually, there is but I don't want to argue with her. For

instance, to be honest, I'm looking forward to being part of the Dog Star because it's the brightest star in our universe (and it has *dog* in it). To be completely honest, I'm not looking forward to the dying part that has to happen first.

I try to make my voice nicer and say, "You must feel really bad. And I'm sorry."

Even with wobbly lips she manages to yell, "Just get in the water, wimp!"

FART!

WIMPs

I'm not upset that Pookie calls me a wimp. And not because I feel bad for her. It's because WIMPs are magical.

No, really. I looked it up.

WIMPs are "weakly interacting massive particles," which are particles smaller than atoms and aren't made up of ordinary stuff like protons and neutrons and electrons. They're called "weakly interacting" because they can actually pass through ordinary stuff without any effect, like a ghost. They're "massive" because they have mass, which means they can be light or heavy although not really heavy because they're so tiny. And they're "particles" because, well, they're particles. I guess physicists can't think of a better word to describe really teeny bits.

WIMPS are like superheroes invisibly passing through other objects.

Also, WIMPS are miraculous because physicists call it a WIMP miracle that they exist at all and behave the way they do. I don't understand the science behind it but I think it's pretty cool that WIMPS are miracles. Like magic!

Here's another cool thing about WIMPS: They're winning the battle against dark energy.

See? WIMPS are magic.

Mr. X calls me back to the dock, but I can only make myself go as far as the edge.

"OK." He sighs. "How about you sit in the water?"

"What!"

"At the edge," he says, walking off the dock and stepping over the rocks to the water lapping at the shore. "Right here."

How we do it is that I sit on the very edge of the lake so just the bottom-est part of my butt gets wet.

Pookie shakes her head at me. "I'm going in after you so don't even THINK of peeing in there!"

I ignore her even though I'm sitting facing her so I don't have to see the lake that's the size of a SUPER MASSIVE BLACK HOLE. But I still know it's there and I can feel its waves trying to drag me in so I quickly stand up to get out but I trip on the slippery rocks and somehow I get water up my nose and I almost drown! I land on the shore, exhausted.

"Wimp!" Pookie yells again.

Mr. X lets me stop swimming after that horrifying experience but only for today because he says otherwise I'll be too scared to ever get back in. I'm already too scared! I've always been too scared! I'm not stupid! I didn't have to almost drown to learn that! *Asciugamano!*

Pookie marches past me to the shore and even though I want to go to my tree room and recuperate I notice the tears on her face and I make myself walk to the edge.

"I'm really, really sorry about that little girl, Pookie. What was her name?"

She grits her teeth. "Cassie."

"Cassie?" I smile. "I can show you the constellation she's in."

Pookie turns to stare at me. "Shut up!"

"No, really. She's probably in Cassiopeia."

"Stop it!" she yells. "Mom! Make him stop!"

But I keep talking. "We're all made of star-stuff, Pookie, and we all go somewhere."

"Mom, come here NOW!" Pookie screams.

"Cassie's got to be up there in—"

"She's dead, Julian! Just dead!"

"No one's just dead! It doesn't happen like that!"

"That's exactly how it happens! It's over."

"No! We stay around! We stay around because people need us! And maybe we need them a little bit, too!"

She looks at me like she's just thought of something big. "OK," she says softly, still staring at me. "OK."

Mom is walking toward us now, giving an exasperated sigh. "What is it?"

"Nothing," we mutter, even though we both know it's not nothing at all.

I can't eat much dinner because my stomach is still too scared about almost drowning. Pookie refuses to eat anything. Mom looks at Joan and grumbles, "I don't know why I even bother."

I feel a lot better after dinner because I find another rock at the bottom of my tree. Mr. X is just going in for the night and I yell over, "Thanks for the rocks, Mr. X!" and I hold up the new one and grin. He squints and says, "Yeah. Nice. I don't get it."

I feel as confused as he looks. But I still love the rocks. Especially this one. It reminds me of the Dog Star because it has a super bright crystal in the middle of the gray.

I even go inside to show it to my family. Maybe it'll brighten their evening, too. And I'm hoping to segue into a conversation about seeing the Dog Star. *Segue* is sort of like *deflect*. In *deflect* you want to change the subject without the other person noticing because you want to get away from the first topic and it doesn't really matter what the second topic is, it's just a distraction. With *segue*, you want to change the subject but you don't really care what the first topic is; it's the second topic that's really important.

I tell them about the rocks I've been getting, maybe from Mr. X, and hold this new one up for them to see. "Look, guys, this shows where the Dog Star is!"

Mom is more impressed with Mr. X than the rock. "I think it shows how much Mr. X cares about you."

Pookie snorts.

Mom glares at her. "It's very special to receive love like that."

"I wouldn't know," Pookie says, all snarly, but I can see her lip quivering before she turns, storms into the pantry, and slams the cupboard door.

Joan rolls her eyes.

Mom sighs.

I clutch my stomach because underneath Pookie being loud and teenager-y, I can uni-sense how much she's hurting. Through the pantry door I see her pick up her empty **DAD** picture frame, and I wish there was a way I could help her fill it.

23

ADOPTION

I'm standing in the water all the way up to my ankles. With BOTH legs. It feels like the water is cold fists around my ankles grabbing tighter and tighter, not letting go, pulling me, dragging me into the water until I scream and manage to break away and run for land, where I fall, shaking but safe.

When I look back at Mr. X he's looking up at the sky, although his eyes are closed.

"Jeez, squirt!" Pookie yells from her lounge chair. "You're so embarrassing!"

Mr. X makes his grumbly sound but I can tell he means it for Pookie, not me. "Come back here," he says quietly.

I do, but I'm not happy about it.

"Where are your goggles?" he says.

"I don't need them."

"Why not?"

"I'm not going underwater."

He grunts. "OK, maybe not today. How about tomorrow?"

"Nope."

"When?"

"When I'm twenty," *because*, I say inside my head, *I may be dead by then*.

He starts to speak but I deflect.

"The dog tag for Sirius is really cool, by the way. It's a beautiful blue, just like the sky."

"Or the water," he says.

"Or the sky," I say back.

"Speaking of the water," he says, "let's swim."

I make a grumbly sound like Mr. X but I try, sort of, to swim. I wade even deeper into the water, up to my knees, but when the water gets beyond my knees it grips so tight I panic. I turn and start to shore, but have you ever tried to run in water? It won't let you run like a normal person, it keeps grabbing your legs and trying to pull you back in. Once you free your knees, the water clutches your calves and once you get your calves clear it grips your ankles even stronger because it's mad that you're escaping. I'm gasping for breath by the time I reach shore, which is ten steps, I counted, but it's the longest ten steps I've taken in my entire life, and I know how Robinson Crusoe felt when he finally got his feet on dry land and kissed the ground. I want to kiss the ground, too, except Pookie is rolling her whole head at me and not just her eyes.

Mr. X lets me take a break and we walk over to his patio.

"Good!" Pookie yells and gets in the lake.

"What's her problem?" Mr. X says.

"She wants her dad."

"Where is he?"

"Our dads were sperm donors who don't want to be identified. Mom has told her that like a kajillion times."

Mr. X's eyebrows go up.

"We come from different dads. We're both from Mom, though. That means—"

"I know what it means." He's holding his hands up in front of his face and turning away like someone just offered him a plate of slugs in liver sauce.

"It's not that big a deal. I hope you're not going to act like some of the kids at school."

He puts his hands down and turns toward me again. "Why? How do they act?"

I imitate their voices. "You're such a freak, Julian. You're the original freak of nature. You're the definition of a freak. You're so freaky—"

"All right, I get the picture. I don't think you're a freak. It's just . . . unusual."

"That's grown-up for freak."

"No."

"Your voice went up at the end. That means you're lying."

"What are you, Homeland Security?"

"There's plenty in life to be worried about, but that's not one of them."

"I stand corrected," Mr. X says. "I apologize."

"It's OK, I still like you."

"Thanks a lot."

"In fact, I like you more because you can admit that you were being stupid."

"Not stupid, just . . . considering."

"You mean, being judgmental."

"Whatever!"

"Anyway, I wish Pookie could see her dad. Then maybe she wouldn't obsess over him all the time."

"Well, if anyone can make that happen, you can."

"Me? I don't think so." I don't know why he would think that. How could I make her dad just appear? I have no idea where he is or even what he looks like.

Mr. X is staring through the patio doors into his living room at the picture with Mrs. X. I look at the walls of pictures he sketched, and that's when I get a brilliant idea.

"Hey, Mr. X, you can draw! Can you draw a picture of Pookie's dad?"

He shrugs. "Do you have a photo of him?"

"No, that's the whole point. It's going to be an amalgamation of all the attributes I can figure out."

"Amalgamation, huh? He'd probably end up looking like Chex Mix. I've never drawn a face without even seeing what a person looks like."

"You can do it, Mr. X. I know you can. If she has a picture maybe she won't obsess about finding him so much. At least she'll have something to put inside her **DAD** picture frame."

"You really care about her, huh?"

"Of course. She's my sister."

He raises his bushy eyebrows at me. "Do you think giving her a picture of her dad will make her like you?"

I shrug. "To be honest, I'm just trying to make life easier on everyone." To be completely honest, which I don't tell him, yes, I wish she'd like me again.

"Look, I'm sorry, I can't draw a picture of someone I don't know. I've only drawn pictures of my wife and my dog. Because I knew them."

"What about your kids?"

"I don't have any kids. I don't like kids. Julia wanted one, but I wasn't around much with my job."

I can uni-sense how much Julia wanted a kid because my heart feels really heavy. "We're not all bad."

He grunts. "Kids are loud and rude and demanding."

"I'm not."

"What about your sister?"

"Well . . . she's not the best example."

He's kind of smirking like he's won the argument so I decide to deflect. "Why weren't you around a lot?"

"I worked at sea."

"On those boats?" I point to the photos on his wall.

"Ships." He looks over at the photos, too.

I walk over to the patio door and make myself look at all the ship pictures. Some of them have a guy who looks like Mr. X only

MUCH younger. One of the pictures catches my eye. It's a young, skinny Mr. X shaking hands with a captain, or some kind of officer with a cap and lots of stripes on his sleeve. And then I notice what's printed below the picture. "Wait. Does that say Merchant Marines?"

"Yeah, I did all kinds of sea work. Merchant Marines was one of them."

"You were in the Merchant Marines, too! Just like Joan! That's magic! Did you ever meet her?"

"No, I would've been retired before she started! Where did she serve?"

"On a boat, I guess."

"It's a ship. And I meant—never mind. Anyway, that's why we didn't have kids."

"That's not a very good reason."

When he looks away, I can feel that there's another reason but he's not saying it. Finally, he shrugs, still staring at her picture. "Julia wanted to adopt but I still didn't want kids, and anyway it's too late now."

"No, it's not. You can adopt me."

He whips around to look at me. "You already have a family."

"Not a granddad."

He looks like he's eaten a sour gummy without meaning to and is looking for somewhere to spit it out. "Julia was the one who wanted kids."

"But she'll know you're adopting me."

"I'm not adopting you, kid!"

"Julian. We know each other too well for you to call me kid.
It's Julian. Like Julia."

And that's when it hits me. "Remember when we were looking
at your boat? And I said the universe was trying to tell us something? Well, now I know what it is . . . I'm your long-lost kid!
That's what the universe is telling us!"

"What?"

"Julia wants you to adopt me!"

"I'm not adopting—"

"OK, not real adopting but adopting like when you get a dog
from the shelter. It's more like getting a friend. Julia wants us to be
friends! And we are. See? You're even trying to teach me to swim.
That's probably what she wanted you to do. That's what friends
do. They help each other. Even if one of them doesn't want that
help. At all. It still makes us friends. Only you're really old so you're
more like a grandfather."

He looks away.

"Which makes me more of a grandson."

"Not really," he says, shaking his head.

"You didn't listen to her before and you feel bad about it.
Maybe you should listen to Julia now."

"Stop calling her Julia!"

"Why? She's my adopted grandmother."

"She's not your adopted grandmother!"

"I bet if you asked her she'd tell you she is."

"I can't ask her! She's not—"

"Yes, she is, too, she's always here and you can talk to her, you just choose not to."

"See, this is why I don't have kids!"

"Maybe if you had kids you'd be smarter."

He starts to answer but I stop him.

"What would Jul—your wife say?"

He looks away because he's avoiding the question.

"You can avoid it all you want," I tell him, "but the universe has thrown us together on purpose and the universe, in this case, is Julia."

He doesn't even yell at me for saying Julia this time. Maybe because he's too busy pinching his nose and swallowing like he's trying to keep the Adam's apple from jumping out of his throat. Which I think means I have a new grandfather.

I find Mom and ask her to get Mr. X a book on how to be a grandfather. Mom is all excited because she thinks Mr. X is having grandchildren.

"No, he doesn't have any kids. Pookie and I are going to be his adopted grandchildren. He just needs a little help in the grandfathering department."

"Oh," she says. "Okayyy," but her forehead is all wrinkled.

"You have found a bookstore, haven't you?" After doctor and major medical facility, independent bookstore is the next most important thing on Mom's list.

"Well, yes, The Briar Patch in Bangor, but I'm not sure when I'm going—"

"You can call them up and order it."

She nods. "Of course. I can do that."

"Thanks, Mom!"

After I've taken care of the book, I write my letter to Mr. X.

Hi, Mr. X,

It's me. Julian. Your adopted grandson.*

Please draw a picture of Pookie's dad for her. I've figured out all of his attributes based on what Pookie didn't inherit from Mom. You're such a good artist and the picture doesn't even have to be that good. It would still mean a lot to her.

I know she's what Mom calls challenging and Joan calls a pain in the butt, but that's because she's hurting inside. I think a picture of her dad would help. Please make it 8 x 10 so it fits in her DAD picture frame.

Here's what Pookie's dad looks like:**

His face is round.

He has dark brown hair.

He has a high forehead.

He has brown eyes.

He has thick eyebrows like yours.

He's thin but maybe not so much because when people get old they're not as thin, just like you're

a LOT thinner in that merchant marine***
photo than you are in the one of you and my
adopted grandmother.

He has a dimple on one side (left) when he
smiles which is probably not a lot, if he's anything
like Pookie, but it's OK to make him smile for the
picture.

Also, you can make him look handsome but not
famous handsome. Unless he looks like Matt Damon.
That would be OK.

Thanks!

Your adopted grandson—just ask Julia,
Julian

*Mom is getting you a book on how to be a
good grandfather. You'll need it because if you're
going to have me as an adopted grandson you
may as well get used to it that you have to
have Pookie as an adopted granddaughter. No
one's saying it's going to be easy.

**If you mess up it's OK because no one knows
what he looks like anyway.

***Isn't it cool how our families have connec-
tions, like you and Joan both being in the
merchant marines? Maybe she'll like you better if
you mention that sometime.

FART!

STELLAR ADOPTION

Sometimes planets get flung out of their star system and are called *rogue* because they don't have a star anymore. They're not rogue on purpose. It just happens. The really cool thing is that another star will sometimes snag that rogue planet and pull it into its orbit, adopting it.

Magic.

24

TURING TEST

It rains for days, which means no swimming lessons! It also means Mr. X isn't out on his patio, and I miss my adopted grandfather. I hope he's working on the drawing of Pookie's dad for his adopted granddaughter. Or maybe he's reading the grandfather book that came yesterday. I left it at his front door and this morning it was gone.

I see a delivery truck come to our house, so I run over from my tree room.

Joan is looking at the card on a big basket of chocolate that's on the kitchen table. And swearing. A lot.

"What's wrong?" Mom asks, getting up from the computer with a grin. "It's chocolate!"

"Sweet old gentleman, huh?" Joan says with a sneer.

"I think so," Mom says. "He reminds me a little of my dad."

"He sounds nothing like your dad! You said your dad was accepting and open."

"It was a different time, Joan, decades ago. He's obviously changed."

Joan rolls her eyes like Pookie.

"He talks to me, doesn't he?" Mom says. "And now he's sending you peace offerings."

"It'll take more than chocolate to buy me," Joan snaps.

"If he can get Julian to—" Mom stops because she sees I'm in the kitchen, but I know what she was going to say: *If he can get Julian to swim . . .*

Joan is gripping the card on the basket and glaring at Mom. "A Merchant Marine? Why would he say I'm a Merchant Marine? Let me guess. It's his way of—"

"Oh, that was me!" I tell her.

Joan glares at me now. "Why would you say that?"

"Because it's true."

"Who told you that?"

I hear a little strangled sound from Mom, but the words are out of my mouth before I can stop them. "Mom. She said that's where you learned to swear."

Joan turns to Mom, in Merchant Marine mode. "The Merchant Marines?"

Mom lets out a little groan. "Uh . . . I guess I was a little frustrated with your swearing once and I . . . sort of . . ."

Turns out that was just an expression. Joan wasn't really in the Merchant Marines. Maybe if she had been she would've liked the lobster.

Mom deflects Joan's glare by saying she's taking me to see my new pediatrician today. That's when I learn something shocking about myself. I'd actually rather be having a swimming lesson with Mr. X. Inconceivable!

The new doctor looks at me and says, "I've never seen this before."

Mom is not happy.

Neither am I.

When it comes to health issues, *Oh, I see this all the time* is much more comforting than, *I've never seen this before.*

On the drive home, Mom says she's embarrassed that I wouldn't even talk to the doctor. But Mom was answering all the questions, so why did I need to talk?

Besides, that's what happens to me in a hospital, emergency clinic, or doctor's office. They all have those fluorescent lights that make everything look gray, even my skin, and they make a hypnotic buzz that Mom says she can't hear but I can, and I get instantly exhausted and I go into a parallel universe until we leave, which is when my skin starts getting its color back and my body warms up and I pass into this universe again.

Mom says I need to be more aware, but some things are too big to think about. I'm already dealing with swimming. It's easier to ignore all the tests, especially since they don't hurt, except drawing blood, but I've gotten used to that. It didn't help that Mom was jumpy and the doctor was serious. It was not a good combination for my stomach, which wanted to throw up the entire time, and I kept telling it to stop or the tests would only go on longer and I wanted to get out of there as fast as possible.

At least there's an awesome package waiting for me at my tree. From Mr. X. The picture of Pookie's dad!

Pookie is walking up from the lake, so I run into the pantry, grab her **DAD** picture frame, and put Mr. X's sketch inside. It looks perfect.

I hear Pookie scream behind me. "Give me that! What are you—" But she stops after grabbing the frame and seeing the picture. Her mouth drops open and her voice turns to a whisper. "What is this?"

"It's your dad. Isn't it cool?"

"But . . . no one knows what my dad looks like."

"I know. It's a composite drawing. Like the police do of criminals."

She narrows her eyes at me.

"I don't mean your dad's a criminal, not that we know of."

Her eyes get squishier.

"I mean, I'm sure he's not." I focus on the picture instead of Pookie. "See, here's your round face. If you look at me and Mom, we have pointier chins, like our faces are upside-down triangles. Yours is a circle. Your dad's must be, too."

She's staring at the picture now. And tracing the line of her dad's chin.

"And Mom's eyebrows are scrawny but yours are normal, so your dad's are probably more like Mr. X's, like caterpillars."

She snorts and kind of smiles at the same time.

"Plus, your hair is darker than mine or Mom's, so that probably comes from your dad."

"How do you know his eyes are brown?"

"It's basic biology. Didn't you take biology? Did you even listen?" I'm starting to think maybe Pookie is the one who needs homeschooling. "Brown eyes are dominant. Mom's are blue. Yours are brown. Your dad's must be brown."

She's staring at her dad's eyes.

"How did you get this?"

"Mr. X drew it for you."

"Why?"

"Because I asked him. And because you're his adopted grand-daughter now."

"What?"

"No, really. Mom even bought him a book on how to be a grandfather. He never got to have kids and he wants them. Well, his wife wants them and he's getting used to the idea."

"His wife is dead."

"But she's still here. She's in the Beehive Cluster of stars in the constellation Cancer. You can see it through my telescope if you want to look."

"Right. And how did she get into the constellation?"

"Automagically."

"You are so weird."

"But in a good way."

"No, in a—"

"I got you a picture of your dad, didn't I?"

She looks at the sketch again and nods. "You did," she whispers. "It's him. Thanks." And she smiles. A real smile.

FART!

TURING TEST

The Turing test is named for Alan Turing, the brilliant British code breaker who helped keep Hitler from winning World War II. Basically, the test is whether you can tell if you're texting with a human or a computer. He figured a computer could be programmed to answer questions in a way that you'd think it was human.

Mr. X's drawing of Pookie's dad is like a paper Turing test. Can you take a bunch of attributes and turn them into a real, live-looking person that someone can believe is her dad? It worked for Pookie. I think Mr. X passed the test.

Alan Turing would be proud of him.

I'm lying in my tree room almost asleep when I hear someone at the base of my tree room. Or maybe I dream it. Or uni-sense it. I blink and see a shadow but I'm not quite awake yet so I'm not sure who I'm seeing. I think it's Mr. X, but then I realize the shadow is moving too fast for Mr. X. And it's going to our house.

It's Pookie.

I shine my flashlight at the bottom of my tree but I don't see anything unusual. I climb down carefully and guess what? I find a rock. Another beautiful rock that looks like the universe.

And I realize that it was never Mr. X who was putting rocks by my tree room. It was Pookie. The whole time. That's why Mr. X was confused when I thanked him for the rocks. That's why Pookie was upset that I thought they were from Mr. X and Mom said it showed how much he cared about me. It was her all along.

And now I don't know whether to thank her or if that'll embarrass her or make her mad. Maybe she wants it to be a secret.

But why would she want to do something nice for me? She hates me.

Or maybe she doesn't. Maybe she really does still love me but she doesn't know how to say it. Maybe rocks are Pookie's language of love.

I go back to bed and think about it some more and even though thinking about Pookie also makes me feel the cauldron on her back, I think the cauldron just got a little lighter.

25

TETRALOGY OF FALLOT

"Come on, kid," Mr. X says with a sigh.

We're standing on the dock and the wind blows off the lake and a dark cloud blocks out the sun and I'm shivering.

"It's too cold."

"It's cool but it's not cold. It's summer in Maine. Now, come on."

I shake my head. "I'm not ready yet."

"Sure you are."

"Nope."

"Just take off the life jacket, will you?"

This is the third day in a row Mr. X has said it's time to take off my life jacket. He says I'll be safe. There's nothing to worry about.

That's hard to believe.

I look over at Pookie in her chair. She's wearing her sunglasses and earbuds and I can hear the music from here, so she wouldn't notice me even if I screamed for help. And is Mr. X strong enough to save me from drowning? He's really, really old.

"Come on, Julian . . . my adopted grandson."

And because he says my name and calls me his adopted grand-son, I decide to try.

I turn away from him and close my eyes. The clasps snap really loudly when I undo them and they echo in my ear. The zipper sounds like a train rushing down the track about to crash. And my heart is beating way too fast and loud. I let my life jacket slip off but I hug my chest to keep from shivering.

Mr. X lets out a swear word but not in an angry way. In a shocked way because he's looking at the scars on my chest, which he can see even though I'm trying to cover them up. "What happened to you?"

"Nothing."

"Nothing?"

"Well, operations."

"Operations?"

"On my heart."

"Your heart?"

I wish he wouldn't repeat everything I'm saying. It's making me nervous. I can tell because I'm shivering more. Or maybe it's getting colder.

"Maybe you shouldn't be swimming."

"T-t-told you."

"Is it bad for your heart? I didn't know. Your mother should've told me! She's a doctor, for—wait a minute . . . not a very good doctor, right?" He starts swearing and pacing on the dock. "Put that life jacket back on!" he barks.

I try to pick it up but I keep dropping it because I'm shaking so much.

"Come on!"

I finally get it and stick one arm in and it takes forever to put the other arm in, and Mr. X's swearing and moaning and pacing isn't helping at all.

It takes seventeen tries to snap the plastic buckle. I counted. When I finally do, it's not a relief at all. In fact, it feels like it's squishing my chest and all the air is coming out of me and none is going in. What's worse, I can't unsnap the buckle now and I can't breathe!

In between gasping for air I'm screaming, but it sounds like someone having voice lessons because I'm shaking so much my screaming comes out all quivery and in short bursts.

Mr. X is swearing at the top of his lungs and that's probably what brings Mom running down to the dock, finally.

She's screaming and swearing louder than both of us . . . about me being blue and can I breathe and do I feel weak and why didn't I call her and I can't seem to say that I WAS calling her and so was Mr. X but I don't think she'd hear me anyway because she's in a complete panic.

Mom shakes Pookie's arm as we pass her. "You were supposed to be watching him!"

Pookie jumps up.

"I'm sorry," Mr. X and Pookie say at the same time, except Mr. X sounds really sorry, and scared, and Pookie just sounds mad.

"He's fine, Mom! Jeez! He's having a panic attack, right, Julian?"

"I guess so," except my voice sounds so strange I say, "Maybe, I don't know."

Actually, I'm feeling a little better now so Pookie's probably right.

"It's OK," I tell Mr. X.

"Are you sure?" he croaks.

"I'm fine."

"See?" Pookie says.

"I'm not taking any chances!" Mom says, dragging me to the car.

I keep trying to squirm out of her grip and run back to Mr. X, who looks panicked, but Mom gets REALLY strong when her adrenaline surges so I just keep yelling back to him, "It's OK! I'm all right! I'm OK!" but it looks like he can't hear me and anyway Mom pushes me into the car and slams the door and all I can do is look out my window and see Mr. X wavering on the dock like he's all ripply and I guess that's when I pass out.

That's how I get to see the barely mediocre (Mom's words) medical facility nearest to our house. I've come to and am feeling much better, except for being in a hospital. Also, Mom's yelling at the emergency room receptionist that she's a doctor and she knows when something is an emergency or not and demands to see the doctor on duty, who is a young guy and Mom treats him like he's Pookie and eventually he starts acting a little like Pookie even though he's a grown-up but he orders tests anyway because

Mom keeps screaming, "Tetralogy of Fallot! Tetralogy of Fallot!" like a crazy person and I have blood tests and an echocardiogram and I don't know what else because I go into a parallel universe and see Rudy who I haven't seen in forever and we ride bikes together that aren't even stationary so it's not that bad.

FART!

TETRALOGY OF FALLOT

It sounds like a cosmic phenomenon, like Transit of Venus, but it's not.

Transit of Venus is when Venus passes between Earth and the sun so it looks like a black dot, or hole, in the sun.

Tetralogy of Fallot is when there's a hole in your heart, plus a lot of other stuff that makes your heart not work right.

Mom says it's not that bad because I will live to be an adult, which I figure means either eighteen or twenty-one depending on whether you think an adult is getting to vote (eighteen) or getting to drink (twenty-one).

You might be thinking, "Hey, you're a smart kid—how come you haven't looked this stuff up before?" Well, here's the answer. Who wants to know when they're going to die? It's like a standardized test. I mean, you know it's coming, you know you can't avoid it, and you know it's going to be bad. The only way to handle it is to try to not think about it at all.

The only problem is this: Sometimes fear gets even huger when you try to pretend it's not there.

Like the elephant in the room.

Sometimes you just have to jump in.

26

LIFE

It's dark by the time Mom and I drive home. She's mad that Joan didn't come to the hospital even though I remind her that we called both Joan and Pookie a kajillion times to let them know what was going on. I pat her shoulder and remind her I'm all right. The tests were fine.

She agrees that the tests were fine, totally fine, all fine, nothing to worry about.

Which makes me start worrying.

As soon as she watches me drink my chocolate milk and gives me a bag of marshmallows and sends me to bed, I hear her calling Joan and whispering, and crying, about the tests.

Mr. X is waiting on his patio and stands up when he sees me.

"It's OK," I lie. "Everything's fine."

I sit on my glider chair and Mr. X sits on his bench, but bolt upright.

It's like we've reversed roles. He's the one who's all anxious and I'm the one who's feeling strangely calm. I'm not even wearing my life jacket, just holding it.

"Is there anything I can do?" he says.

"You already have."

"But I haven't even taught you to swim."

I shrug. "I'll probably swim. Some day."

"I wish I could've done more."

"You've been my friend. You listened when no one else would. And . . ."

"And what?"

"And maybe you can see the magic in the universe?"

"I don't know about that. How would that help you, anyway?"

"We're all connected. Whether it's in this life or up in the stars. Or in parallel universes. You've got to see that."

He nods.

"I have to go now. There's some stuff I need to take care of. With my family."

He nods like he really understands. I know he does.

"Bye, Mr. X."

"Bye, Julian."

I head down to the lake to see Pookie, who's sitting on the dock under the stars.

"Wait!" Mr. X calls.

I turn around.

He's standing up, wavering. "Will we see each other again?"

"Of course," I tell him. "It'll just be in a parallel universe. See ya, Mr. X."

"See ya . . . grandson." He smiles. A whole smile. And I grin back at him.

I get to the edge of the dock and call out to Pookie.

"Oh, you're back. So . . . panic attack, right?"

"I think so."

"I figured."

"But . . . well, I came to say goodbye."

"Where are you going?"

"I think I'm going to die pretty soon."

She rolls her eyes. "And they call ME the drama queen!"

"No, really. Did Mom tell you what's wrong with me?"

"That would take a week, squirt."

"I'm serious. I mean the, you know."

She cocks her head. "Do *you* know?"

"Sort of, except she hides it from me."

"She doesn't want you to worry. If you ask me, she blows it out of proportion. You're fine."

I don't answer and her voice changes.

"Aren't you?"

"I had some tests at the hospital."

"And?"

"And she called Joan and was crying on the phone and she gave me these and said I could eat them all." I hold up the marshmallows for Pookie to see.

She grabs the bag and looks at it more closely. "Joan must've bought these. They're not even organic."

"I know."

Pookie swallows. "This wasn't supposed to happen for a long time."

"*What* wasn't supposed to happen?"

She stands up fast. "I can't believe they wouldn't tell me!"

"Tell you *what*?!"

Joan's Outback skids into the driveway, spraying gravel everywhere, and Joan leaps out, taking the front stairs two at a time.

Pookie grabs me by my life jacket except I'm not wearing it anymore, just holding it, and we run to the house like we're in some weird relay race where neither of us will let go of the baton life jacket.

Joan is reading the letter from the hospital, saying, "It says increased risk of—oh! Hi, kiddos," she says when she sees us march in.

"Don't *hi, kiddos* us!" Pookie yells. "He's my brother and why didn't you keep me in the loop?"

It's silent now except my heart that's pounding and I want to say, "Why didn't you keep ME in the loop?" but my throat is closed up and I'm having enough trouble just breathing.

Pookie makes a croaking sound and her voice is whisper-shout-y and cracking. "This is so unfair! I can't believe you two! I would've been nicer to him if you'd told me he was going to die *now*!"

I gulp as much air as I can. "I'm going to die *now*?"

"Of course not!" Joan says, but Mom gulps a sob and I don't know which one of them to believe.

"Tell me the truth!" Pookie yells the words right out of my brain.

"Your mother is overreacting." Joan sounds so sure I almost, I want to, believe her. She looks at Mom. "Really, Michelle, did you even read the whole thing?" Joan reads the letter out loud, but I can't follow because the words come out too fast and they're too medical and my ears are too nervous.

"So what does it mean?" Pookie says when Joan finishes.

"It means we have to be careful, like always, but there's nothing new to worry about."

Joan and Pookie glare at Mom. Mom starts to say something, but I finally open my mouth and speak first. "You mean, I can still live until I'm eighteen? Or maybe twenty-one?"

"What?" Joan says. "You have until fifty or sixty, at least."

"Fifty?" I say.

"Or older," Mom says, glaring at Joan. "They might come up with a complete cure."

I stare at them. "Fifty is ancient!"

"I wouldn't say ancient," Joan mutters.

"Joan!" Mom barks. She turns to me. "Did you really think you would die so young?"

"Yes!"

"Why?"

"Because you always go into a panic like I'm about to die!"

"We just wanted to keep you safe," Mom says, "because there are risks with tetralogy of Fallot. That's why you can't play contact sports and you have to take antibiotics and we don't want you to get too stressed and—"

"Why did you have to whisper all the time? That made it really scary, like it was so bad you couldn't tell me!"

Mom looks at Joan, who folds her arms and raises her eyebrows, before looking back at me. "We—I just didn't want you to worry."

"Well," says Pookie, "that obviously backfired."

"I always said it would be fine," Joan points out.

Pookie snorts. "But when you say that, it's never fine."

"That's not true!" Joan says.

"What about drama camp, huh? It'll be fine. Guess what? The drama camps are probably full for the rest of the season! And Mom ditching her career was going to be temporary? It'll be fine? And what about this B&B disaster? It'll be fine?"

The arguing continues after I escape to my tree room until Pookie slams doors in the pantry so it's just Mom and Joan whisper-shouting with Mom saying stuff like, "Pookie can just—" and then whispering, and Joan saying, "I can't live with her—" and then whispering, and then I hear my name and Mom saying, "Well, I'm going to go talk to that doctor right now and make sure!" and Joan answering, "Fine! I'm going to finish the last thirty minutes of my shift so I can actually get paid!"

I hear Mom's van door slam and she peels out of the driveway.

The Outback door slams right after and Joan drives off, too.

I look down at Mr. X's patio but he's not there. I guess I knew he wouldn't be but I miss him now.

I go down the ladder and over to my telescope because that always makes me feel good. I feel REALLY good that I'm not going to die when I'm eighteen or twenty-one but instead not until I'm ancient. I just wish my family would stop arguing so much. And I realize I still haven't gotten my family to look through my telescope. Maybe I'll just have to find a comet first.

This could be the night.

It feels like something very special—super massively huge!—is about to happen and even my telescope lens seems clearer, like I can see, I mean really see, for the first time ever. This is the night of discovery!

FART!

ORION NEBULA

It's an awesomely clear night so I look through my telescope at Orion and see the nebula where stars are born. It looks like a bird with wispy wings flying through the universe.

Magic.

27

THE END OF ORION

I see Pookie peek out the kitchen door and I call her over. "Come on! Come see this!"

She hesitates at the door, then marches over.

Finally! Someone will actually look through my telescope!

Except she looks a little mad so I decide to cheer her up first. "Isn't it cool that I'm not about to die? I can't believe it!"

"Mom can't, either. That's why our entire lives revolve around you. It's like you're the sun and we all orbit you but you're about to explode so we have to hold our breath."

I laugh.

Pookie doesn't.

"That's the way everyone feels around *you*," I tell her.

"Me? I'm not even a part of this family. And I can't wait to be out of here. Neither can they."

"What do you mean?"

"Seriously? Didn't you hear Joan say she can't stand living with me?"

"I couldn't hear what she was saying," I lie, "but I'm sure she didn't mean that."

"Yes, she does. Even Mom would like to get rid of me, and she's my own mother."

"They could get rid of you if they wanted but they don't."

"They can't because I'm not eighteen yet. Believe me, if they could they'd dump me in a heartbeat. We're not even a family."

"Yes, we are." I say what Mom always tells us. "Your family is the people around you who love you."

She shakes her head. "I bet my father wouldn't be trying to get rid of me."

"Maybe if you didn't say that all the time they'd like you better. It's like being at a friend's house and saying you'd rather be at another friend's house because you like them better."

"You just don't get it, do you? Everything's about you. Changing our lives completely to suit your needs. Mom quits work so she can homeschool you. We move to this deadwater so there's no stress on little Julian and you can use your telescope every night."

"Mom wanted to move."

"Maybe. Did you ever think it might be all because of you?"

"Not really."

"That's because we've trained you to think of nothing but yourself."

"That's not true! I don't just think about me! I worry about you guys all the—"

"It's not your fault. We treat you like the crown prince, so of course you think the world revolves around you."

"No, I don't!"

"I bet even Mr. X is just humoring you."

I can feel my face turn red and my muscles tighten up and my eyes narrow like Pookie's.

"He's your only friend and Mom probably told him to be."

My teeth are clenched but I manage to spit out, "Mom did not tell him."

"Seriously, Julian, who actually likes you? Have you ever had a friend?"

I'm breathing fast and my heart is pounding really hard, which, even though I'm not about to die, is still not good for it.

"Other than Mom and Joan, I mean? Do you ever even wonder about your father? Or is having two planets orbiting you enough? Three if you count Mr. X, although he's really just a shadow planet."

"Shut up!"

She raises her eyebrows because it's usually her telling me to shut up.

"At least I'm not a pain in the butt like you are!"

"Is that what our parents say?"

"Well, you are! I bet your precious dad would even say that!"

Her face turns into the Princess of Darkness. "Don't you ever say anything about my dad. You have no idea about our relationship."

"You don't have a relationship!"

"Shut up!" she barks.

"He doesn't even know who you are!"

"I said shut up!" Her voice is all scream-y, but I just raise my voice louder.

"He probably doesn't know you exist!"

"How dare you!"

"And if he did know you he probably wouldn't even like you! He'd probably—"

A colossal orangutan noise bursts from deep inside her and she screams and shoves my telescope and I see a giant flash from my dying telescope as it hits the ground with a crunch, and the eyepiece and plastic pieces break off like they're parts of an exploding star.

And even though I'm the one who should be crying, Pookie explodes into tears and hiccup-sobs all the way back to the pantry.

I crouch over the pieces of my Orion XT8 telescope and pick up some of the parts even though I know it can't be fixed. I can't even believe it happened. I feel like I'm seeing the shock wave of a supernova explosion from a distant galaxy.

FART!

SUPERNOVA

Supernova—the catastrophic event of an exploding star.

28

VOYAGER

"What happened?" Joan is staring at what used to be my telescope.

"Pookie and I had a fight."

She looks at me. "About?"

"She says I'm the sun in our family and everyone else revolves around me. It's all about me and that's why we moved to Maine."

"That's not true. We moved to Maine for a lot of reasons. One of them was Pookie."

"Pookie?"

"She was getting in with the wrong crowd."

I stare at her.

"I know. You can't escape your problems by moving." She sighs. "We wanted a quieter place and a calmer life for all of us."

"Somebody should probably tell her that, because she blames me."

"Sorry, kiddo. I didn't mean for you to be left holding the bag."

I shrug. "It's not as heavy as your bag. Or Mom's. Or even Pookie's cauldron."

"Excuse me?"

"Never mind. It's just an expression. Like Merchant Marines. Sort of. Only more confusing."

"You got that right," she says. "To be honest, I wasn't a hundred percent behind this idea, but it was important to your mother."

"Like homeschooling me?"

"I don't think that's necessary. I did figure you'd love it here, though."

"I do. Except not so much at the moment." And I tell her the horrible thing I said to Pookie about her dad probably not even liking her. I even tell her that Pookie heard her say that Joan can't handle her anymore.

"When did I say that?"

"Tonight. You said, 'I can't live with her,' and then you whispered so we couldn't hear the rest."

"I said I can't live with her missing drama camp! I spent my last paycheck to sign her up, plus the late fee, and your mother was mad at me about it. She figured Pookie could wait until next year."

"Really? You were doing something nice?"

"Is that such a surprise?"

"Well, sometimes you guys are kind of . . . harsh with Pookie."

"There's a history there."

"I know. I mean, I don't know what it is, but you guys are still mad at her."

Joan swears.

"So-rry."

"No, I'm just mad at myself again. We need to handle this better. I do love your sister even though she's aggravating. Believe it or not, there's a lot I want to say that I don't, like when she threatens to run away I really want to say, 'Please! I'll get the suitcase for you!' but I don't."

I look over at the house. "Uh-oh."

"What?"

I run to the pantry.

"Julian! What's wrong?"

I'm running too fast to answer. I push through the kitchen door and into the pantry. I have to see if . . . Oh, no!

Joan is behind me. "Where is she?"

"Her dad picture is gone. Her KEEP OUT bag is gone." I turn around to face Joan. "Pookie's gone."

Joan swears, closes her eyes, and holds her head for a moment. When she drops her hands she's Merchant Marine Joan. "OK, I'm going to find your sister. I'll call your mother and tell her what's happened. She can take a different route and look for her."

"I'll come with you," I say.

"No. If Pookie comes back somebody should be here. Is Mr. X around?"

"Yes." It's not really a lie. He's around *some*where. Even if it's in a parallel universe.

"Good. If you need anything, go see Mr. X."

"OK," I say, even though I can't. It doesn't matter. All I want is for Joan to hurry up and find Pookie.

After she leaves, I realize she ran off so fast she didn't leave me her phone. I guess she needed it, but we don't have a landline. And Mr. X really isn't here. I'm totally alone.

I go back out to my telescope, or my ex-telescope, and just stand there. I look up at the sky with my naked eye and stare for a while. Even without my telescope I can see a kajillion stars. I start counting them, hoping that Joan will find Pookie before I finish. I talk to Granddad in the Wild Duck Cluster, and to Mrs. X in Cancer. I wish Mr. X were here with me now. I really miss him. And I miss Pookie. Even though she smashed my telescope. I don't want her gone forever.

I don't know how long I'm standing there, staring at the sky, before I see it. A shooting star. It's the first one I've ever seen in real life. My heart is pounding and I can't help saying, "Wow!" as I watch it arc over the lake to the other side. Where the grotto with the BVM is. And that's when I know where Pookie went. To see Trey and his Camaro. I have to stop her.

If you need anything, go see Mr. X, Joan said.

So I do.

Mr. X might not be here, but I remember he has something that can help me.

It's not a phone.

It's a boat.

FART!

VOYAGER 1

Voyager 1 is the only spacecraft to go interstellar, exiting the power of our sun.

29

LAUNCH

I don't even stop long enough to leave a note for Mom and Joan.

I do stop for one thing—to put my life jacket back on.

I'm not stupid.

When I get the boat to the lake I make a shocking discovery. Stars are shining back at me from the water. The whole universe is perfectly reflected. Of course! The universe is in everything! I *knew* that, but why didn't I think of it before? The universe was here all along, staring at me, at all of us.

I push off from the shore and climb in.

Here's something else I always knew about the universe. It's powerful and chaotic and massive and frightening.

Just like the lake.

I try really hard not to have another panic attack.

Asciugamano!

Then I remember I'm learning Spanish.

Hola! I like marshmallows. *Me gusta* . . . marshmallows.

What is *marshmallow* in Spanish? OK, see, I can't die yet

because I have to live long enough to look that up, so I can't fall apart now.

Plus, I have to find my sister, *mi hermana*.

That's what I'm doing here.

In the lake.

In a Styrofoam boat.

I have to find Pookie.

Mr. X is right that a rowing machine does not make you an expert at rowing an actual boat. For one thing, there's *water* under a boat. A LOT of water. The water fights you. It jostles you and makes you turn in different directions, sometimes even circles.

And it makes you throw up. I puke in the water. More than once. "Sorry, fish," I croak, every time.

You have to keep looking where you're going and not let the water take over. It's OK to scream if a little water makes it into your boat because that is shocking. It doesn't make the boat sink, though. It just makes your butt wet. And you keep rowing.

I can hear Mr. X's voice far away saying, *Live, Have to live, You have to live*, and even though his voice is soft and hard to hear over my breathing because I'm panicking—I mean REALLY panicking—his voice is insistent and keeps saying, *You have to live* over and over like a mantra, the same mantra I said to him before I even knew him, and he keeps repeating it until I start saying it, too, first in my head and then in my mouth and I say it louder and louder until I'm shouting it so loud I feel like Mr. X can hear me and then I know he can because I uni-sense him smiling and even though his eyes are closed I can hear his brain saying, *You have to live* like we're experiencing a Vulcan mind meld. And I feel calmer even though I'm hyperaware that this is still an emergency situation.

I'm even starting to get the hang of rowing a Styrofoam boat and not be too panicked, sort of, as long as I keep saying my mantra, *You have to live, You have to live.*

Until the shipwreck.

I don't know what happened. I just know I'm in the water and I'm completely wet and the cold is seeping under my life jacket clutching my chest so I can hardly breathe and someone is screaming so loudly it hurts my ears and when I close my mouth to keep the water from coming in the screaming stops.

You have to live

So, OK, the screaming was me.

You have to live

That's when I can hear the sloshing in my ears.

You have to live

I focus on the fact that I'm floating in the water and not drowning in the water.

You have to live

I keep saying my mantra.

And then I start panting because it's hard to breathe.

You have to live

Until something touches my leg and I don't mean water. It scratches once, then scratches again and I can't help screaming. I kick my legs and wave my arms, splashing, and I hit something.

A tree branch.

Of a tree leaning over the water.

From the shore.

I grab it and somehow pull myself onto dry land. Or maybe wet-land but at least it's out of the lake and all I can hear is my breathing.

You have to live

It's so loud and weird it sounds like I'm speaking orangutan.

That's when I remember Pookie and why I'm here.

You have to live

And I make myself get up onto my wobbly legs and walk.

FART!

ESCAPE VELOCITY

Escape velocity—the speed needed to escape the gravitational pull of a planet.

30

LANDING

"Are you lost, kid?" At first I think he's a Mountie but then I realize I'm not in Canada even though it feels like I've traveled forever. He just has a cool hat. Plus, his police car has a badge that says SHERIFF'S OFFICE MAINE.

"I'm not lost. Well, a little bit. I'm on a mission."

"A mission?"

"My sister ran away and it's all my fault."

"Where are your parents?"

"Out looking for her."

"And I bet you were supposed to stay home. Why are you all wet?"

"I had a shipwreck." I shiver, and not just because I'm cold and wet. "But let's not talk about that right now. I have to find my sister."

"OK, let's start with a description of the little girl."

"She's not that little. She's fourteen."

"She's your big sister? Why are you out looking for her?"

"I told you. Because–"

"OK, never mind. Get in the car."

I run to the front seat, slam the door, and put on my seat belt.

The cop is getting something out of his trunk and moves like he's walking through water.

"Come *on*, already!"

I can't believe I just yelled at a cop, but he does actually speed up.

He hands me a blanket, which is I guess what he was getting out of the trunk. I want to say, "I didn't need a blanket! Just go!" but then I realize I'm shivering so I say, "Thanks" instead.

Officer Marty radios the information about a missing teen as I tell him all about Pookie and my telescope and Mr. X and how I thought Pookie was throwing rocks at us like the Oort Cloud but really she was collecting them and giving them to me to make up for being the dark energy that takes up our entire universe, and how stressed my parents are all the time and that I hope when they say, "I've had just about enough of this!" they don't really mean it because Pookie is very, well, *challenging*, but she doesn't mean to be, it's just what happens to people when they become teenagers and their brains explode, and I also tell him that Cassie died and now that I think of it Mom shouldn't have made Pookie work at a camp for dying children since her own brother was dying except that now I'm not, actually, which is good, and how Trey at the grotto with the BVM probably gave her a ride somewhere because he read her butt.

Marty growls, and I say, "I know!" because it's exactly how I felt when Trey read her butt.

He does a U-turn right in the middle of the road, which is really scary except it's Maine, not DC, so there aren't any actual cars in the way.

Marty growls again and radios for someone to track down Trey and his Camaro ASAP.

My heart is beating faster and I want to ask if Trey is dangerous but Marty is still on the radio, saying he's headed for the bus station in Bangor in case Trey took her there, which I hope is what happened because I really, really don't want her stuck in his car.

I feel exhausted and now that the crackling of the radio is quiet I suddenly feel empty and the emptiness is crushing me like a black hole.

"Is she going to be OK?" I whisper and I can feel the words turn to liquid and spill out of my eyes.

"We're not losing any kid on my watch," he says and turns on his lights and sirens and pushes the go pedal to the floor, and I feel like we're in a spaceship traveling at the speed of light; at least, I hope so, because I want to get to Pookie before she has a chance to go to a parallel universe.

Marty wants to call my mom and tell her I'm OK but I guess I'm panicking because I can't remember her number. I can't believe it!

"I remember Joan's number, though," and I tell him what it is.

"Who's Joan?"

"She's my mom, too."

"Good," Marty says, and he actually sounds relieved—his shoulders even relax a little. "I don't think one mom is enough for you and your sister."

FART!

APOLLO 13

We speed so fast in the night with the blue lights flashing in the dark that I feel like I'm in a rocket hurtling through space and I think about Apollo 13 again and I hope that three people's wishes, if they're really big and powerful, can bring Pookie back.

If that doesn't work I hope I'm in a parallel universe that's moving faster than Pookie's so I can catch her.

31

RECOVERY

We scream into the bus station and jump out of the car and run inside to the counter and Marty finds out that a possible juvenile fitting Pookie's description just boarded the bus for DC and it's pulling out now.

He yells, "Stay put!" as he runs for his patrol car but I run the other way. I know where the bus is. I uni-sense Pookie inside it. I chase after it, cry-shouting, "Don't leave, don't leave, don't leave!"

I know she can't hear me. No one can. It's like shouting into a black hole after someone has disappeared and is never coming out again.

All I can see is black smoke and red lights like red dwarf stars getting farther and farther away.

And then I see a face.

Pressed against the back window.

With big wide eyes and an open mouth.

Pookie.

Suddenly, blue lights are flashing and a siren is screaming and just when I think the bus is going to disappear around a turn and never come back it lurches to a stop. I keep running because it still feels so far out of my reach.

The door opens and Pookie shoots out of there, running like she's escaping a black hole, toward me, even dropping her KEEP OUT bag so she can run faster. She picks me up and holds me tight and swings me around like she did when I was little only now we're not laughing, we're crying, and I'm gulping, "I'm sorry, I'm sorry, I'm sorry," and she's gulping, "Me too, me too, me too!"

"How did you get here?" she asks when she finally puts me down. Then she realizes something. "Are you wet? What happened?"

"Shipwreck."

"What?"

"I lost Mr. X's boat. But I'll buy him another one. It was only Styrofoam."

She looks stunned.

"Really. It's—it was—Styrofoam."

"You got in the water? In a boat? By yourself?"

I nod.

"Across the whole lake?"

I nod again.

"For me?"

I'm nodding so much I feel like a bobblehead.

She picks me up again and squeezes me so tight I'm vibrating. And then I realize it's Pookie crying.

I hear a cough nearby and look over to see Marty.

"Kids, your folks are on their way. Do you have all your luggage, young lady?"

Pookie is too busy crying so I point at her backpack on the road and nod.

He goes to pick it up and waves at the bus driver, who's looking out the door. "You can go on!" Marty says. "She's home."

And when I hear that I hug her back just as tight. "Thanks for the rocks. I know it was you."

She stops hugging me so she can look at me. "I didn't mean what I said about Mr. X. I'm sure he likes you."

"I didn't mean that about your dad, either. I'm sure he likes you, too."

She swallows hard and nods. I know she still misses him. Or the idea of him.

"We're still a family," I tell her, "even though it's just you and me and Mom and Joan."

"I know."

"And it's true what Mom says, that family is the people around you who—"

"Love you," she says, "yes, I know," but she doesn't sound convinced.

"They may not act like it, but they really love you. For instance, tonight Joan wasn't saying she couldn't live with you, she was saying she couldn't live with you not getting to go to drama camp because it wasn't fair."

Her mouth drops open. "Really?"

I nod. "And she spent all her money so you could go to the last session."

Tears spill out of Pookie's eyes.

"We all love you, Pookie. And . . . you love us, too, right?"

"Of course. Don't be stupid, stupid." She looks away and I uni-sense that she wishes she hadn't said that, it's just the way she's been used to acting.

So I poke her. "Don't be stupid, *stupid*? Isn't that an oxy-moron, *moron*?"

And we both smile.

She hugs me again. "I can't believe Mr. X would let you go out on a boat!"

"He wasn't there," I say softly.

"Alone!" Pookie continues. "What was he thinking?!"

"He wasn't there," I say louder, but my words are muffled in her stomach because she's hugging me so tight.

"How could he do that? Why would—"

"He wasn't there, Pookie!" I push back from her so she can hear me. "He wasn't there!"

She stops and stares at me, but her eyes aren't squinty. They're wide open.

Behind Pookie, a bus is roaring toward the station, lighting her up like she has a halo, and Marty hits his siren and puts on his high beams and flashing lights, spinning blue and white and it's so bright I almost can't look at Pookie. It's like a quasar is coming out of her head.

When my eyes finally adjust, her face looks different and her eyes are the Pookie I used to know, only a little different but not in a mean or scary way.

"Mr. X wasn't there?" Pookie says.

I shake my head.

"Do Mom and Joan know?"

"I just told Joan he was around."

"You lied to her?"

"It's kind of true. He's around in a parallel universe."

She looks at me like Mr. X does, like she's looking into the prefrontal cortex of my brain.

"Is Joan going to be mad?" I ask her. "And Mom?"

She thinks for a moment. "You did what you needed to do."

"But . . . do you think they'll understand?"

"It's OK," she says. "I understand. I'll explain it to them."

"Thanks," I say slowly, but I wonder if she understands *all of it.*

"Yes," Pookie says, "*all of it.*"

She knows what I'm thinking again! Pookie knows. I hug her tight and feel so relieved it's like the universe itself is sighing.

FART!

QUASAR

Quasar—the brightest light in the universe, emitted from black holes.

32

· HEART ·

Mom runs to Pookie and grabs her. "Oh, honey! Thank good-ness you're OK!"

Joan looks at me. "How did you get here?"

That's when Mom notices me. "Is Mr. X here?"

"Not exactly."

"Julian swam across the lake to find me," Pookie says.

"What?" Mom and Joan say together.

"Not swam!" I point out. "I took the boat and then—"

"What boat?" Joan says.

"Mr. X's boat. I know how to row from the rowing machine at the station, remember?"

"You rowed a boat by yourself—"

"Until the shipwreck."

Mom screams.

"It's OK! I'm fine. See?"

Joan speaks slowly. "Where was Mr. X?"

"He wasn't there, exactly."

"You told me—"

"I know, but it wasn't exactly true."

Mom finally lets go of Pookie so Joan can hug her.

"Come here, kiddo," and Joan gives her a huge, long hug and I think she's forgotten about me and the whole Mr. X thing but when she stops hugging Pookie and Mom takes over, she turns back to me.

"So where is Mr. X, then?"

"Well—" And that's when it happens. A searing pain rips through my heart and I bend over.

"Julian?" Joan says.

My heart is squeezing and hurting so much I can't breathe. I feel like I'm going to faint. But this time it's not a panic attack. It hurts way too much.

"Julian!" Mom screams. "Call 911!"

Joan is already on her phone and talking to me at the same time. "Dizzy? Chest pressure?"

I nod.

"Heart attack," she says into the phone. "Hurry! He has a heart condition, tetralogy of Fallot."

Mom is screaming, Joan keeps talking into the phone, and Pookie is leaning down with her arms around me, whisper-crying, "You have to live! You have to live! You have to live!"

And the mantra starts in my head, too, *You have to live, You have to live, You have to live*, and I think about Mr. X talking me across the lake with *You have to live* just so I could save Pookie and even though I don't want to die yet I'm grateful he got me here so I could bring my family together.

You have to live, You have to live.

I keep saying the mantra and wishing my family really knew how to find the Dog Star, *You have to live, You have to live*, and hoping that Mr. X will find the Beehive Cluster and talk with Mrs. X, *You have to live, You have to live*, and I wonder which star Mr. X will end up in, and as soon as I think of Mr. X and his star my heart squeezes so much I stop breathing.

And that's when I realize something.

It's not me who's dying.

It's Mr. X.

"Mr. X," I manage to whisper to Pookie. "It's Mr. X!"

Pookie stops crying and stares at me for just a split second before whirling around and grabbing Mom's phone, tapping it and holding it up to Joan. "This is the address! St. Petersburg, Florida!"

"What?" Joan says.

"Mr. X! He's the one having the heart attack! Not Julian!"

"Are you sure?" Joan asks.

"Yes!" Pookie yells.

"Yes!" I whisper-scream, still clutching my heart because it hurts so much.

You have to live, You have to live, You have to live. I squeeze my eyes tight and uni-sense to Mr. X that the ambulance is coming and he's going to be OK. *You have to live, You have to live, You have to live.*

"Julian!" Mom is still screaming.

"He's fine!" Pookie yells. "Just call!"

Joan barks into the phone that she needs 911 for St. Petersburg, Florida. "Heart attack," Joan says. "Elderly man."

"Hurry!" Pookie and I say at the same time.

You have to live, You have to live, You have to live

I keep saying it over and over until my heart starts beating normally and without pain and I breathe out a big sigh and Joan says, "The ambulance is there! They've got him!" and I say, "I know."

FART!

PARALLAX

Parallax—the apparent change in position of two objects viewed from different locations.

33

SHOCK WAVE

Mom insists that the ambulance check me out. My EKG is fine and Joan talks with the paramedics because she knows them. She also thanks Marty and he shakes hands with me and has a private conversation with Pookie where she's nodding her head a lot and the only thing I hear is at the end when Marty says, "And tell your moms to buy you a new pair of shorts." Pookie looks down at her jeans and then back to Marty, but he's already getting in his patrol car so I'll have to explain that to her later.

Joan gets off the phone and says, "Mr. X is at the hospital and he's doing fine. It looks like he's going to be OK. But how did you know he was having a heart attack?"

"I could feel it."

"Did he say anything about heartburn or a sore arm or headache or anything?"

I shake my head. "I just knew."

Mom nods slowly like she's taking it in and maybe even believing it. "Pookie," she says, "how did you know he was in Florida?"

"Yes," Joan says, "I'd like to hear this, too."

"Because," Pookie says, "that's where he lives."

Mom throws her hands in the air. "Except when he's next door!"

I moan, but Pookie takes my hand and squeezes it gently. "Mr. X has never been next door."

FART!

SHOCK WAVE

Shock wave—a pressure wave produced by an explosion such as a supernova.

34

SCIENCE MAGIC

"I'm confused," Joan says.

"You mean, he goes back and forth to Florida all the time," Mom explains.

Pookie shakes her head. "No. I mean he's been in Florida the whole time. He's never been here."

"Of course he has," Mom says. "Julian has been spending the entire summer—"

"Right," Pookie interrupts, "Julian. Has anyone else seen Mr. X?"

Mom and Joan look at each other and slowly shake their heads.

"Wait," Joan says, "are you saying Mr. X is an imaginary friend? Because that's impossible. Did Julian think up Mr. Hale?"

"Really, Pookie," Mom says, "I talk with him on the phone all the time."

"Exactly," Pookie says, "never in person, though, right?"

"Well, no, but . . . but I've been talking to him . . ."

"Right, Mom," Pookie says slowly, like she's explaining something to a little kid, "you've been talking to him. On the phone. Where he lives. In Florida."

"But . . . then"—Mom looks at me—"how do they know things about each other?"

Pookie shrugs. "You've told him all about Julian, I'm sure."

"That's true," Mom says, her forehead crinkling, "and Julian has written him several letters."

"OK," says Joan, "that explains how Mr. X knows about Julian, but how could Julian know anything about Mr. X?"

I'm just starting to feel strange that people are talking around me like I'm the elephant in the room when Joan turns to me and repeats her question. "How do you know anything about Mr. X?"

Pookie answers for me. "He just does. He's like that."

"Julian?" Joan demands.

"I want to hear this, too," Mom says.

"Well . . . I looked inside his house. I saw the pictures on the wall of him and Mrs. X and his dog and the ships he was on. I saw his boat in the garage. I knew he was sad. Mr. Hale even said that—his wife died, he'd given up on life and was a broken old man. I could feel that. He was lonely. And needed a friend. I understood. Plus, I'm a uni-sensor, remember."

Mom is staring at me. "You spent all that time with him but he was never actually there?"

"Well, you guys weren't listening to me."

Now instead of Mom and Joan acting almost mad they look at each other like they forgot to go to a parent-teacher conference.

Joan closes her eyes and puts her hands on her head like she's trying to keep her head from exploding. "But you never had any actual communication with him? I can't believe this!"

"Science doesn't care if you believe in it or not," Pookie says.

Whoa! She's actually sort of almost paraphrasing Neil deGrasse Tyson! Magic!

Joan stares at Pookie. "It's not science!"

"How do you know? Maybe it is." Pookie raises her eyebrows at me and smiles. "Parallel universes?"

I smile back at her and nod because she's exactly right.

Joan is still holding her head together. "Michelle, did you give Julian information about Mr. X?"

Mom shakes her head. "No. Not at all. I—I just can't believe this."

"That's why it doesn't happen to you, Mom," I explain, "because you don't believe. You have to be open to the magic to feel it."

"So," says Joan, taking her hands off of her head and sitting down, "it's like an imaginary friend?"

"Not imaginary. I just haven't actually met him yet. I've been spending time with him in a parallel universe."

Mom and Joan stare at me.

Pookie rolls her eyes. "Why is this so hard for you guys to understand? He's always been like this. He can see and feel things other people can't. It's the magic of Julian."

I smile at Pookie. I'm feeling warm and happy because she actually understands me again. She didn't forget. She didn't completely change. The good part of her is still there.

I go over to her and give her a hug and she hugs me back in a way that means, *OK, I guess I've been a pain but that's over now and let's move forward.*

Mom throws her hands in the air again and comes over to hug us both. "Well, the important thing is we're all together."

"Yes," Joan says, "one big happy—crazy—family!"

We're in one big happy, crazy hug with me in the middle and even though my arms are squished against my sides so I can't hug back it still feels like magic. My heart is all warm and grinny but I take the time to send a special kindness meditation to Mr. X with a different last line which goes like this:

May your life unfold with inner ease and grace onto a plane to come visit us really soon.

FART!

PARALLEL UNIVERSE

Parallel universe—a coexisting universe that mirrors our own.

35

SURPRISES

A couple of days later we're in the kitchen when Mr. X calls Mom from the hospital. Mom puts him on speaker. He sounds weak and old but he's OK. And when he gets better he's going to visit. In the meantime, he says he's dropping the lawsuit about wrecking our addition.

"Oh, that's so nice of you!" Mom says. "Are you sure you want to do that?"

Joan glares at Mom so hard I can hear the *Shut up* coming out of her eyes.

"I owe my life to your son," Mr. X says. "I can live with the addition."

"I'm sorry about your boat," I say.

"That's OK, kid," he says, and I grin, because he sounds exactly the same in this universe as he did in the other one.

"You can help me build another one. And then you can get in the water with it."

I'm not grinning anymore because now he sounds TOO much like the other Mr. X. "That's OK, I don't—"

"I'm not taking no for an answer."

Joan is chuckling. A nurse tells Mr. X he has to get off the phone so we say goodbye.

I tell Joan I don't want to get in a boat again. I mean, I know I've done it but it was not the best of experiences, especially the shipwreck part.

Joan shrugs. "That's one way Mr. X and I are the same. We don't take no for an answer."

She's right because I try saying *No*, a lot, but Joan won't accept it. She says the whole boat experience will be just great.

Mom raises her eyebrows at Joan. "What about Mr. X's other plan?"

Joan is not smiling anymore. "That's a definite no."

"What plan?"

Joan walks off.

Mom sighs and tells me what it is. Sirius. "Mr. X has pretty much convinced me," she says, "but not Joan."

"Why not? That's so unfair!" I can't help sounding a little whiny.

Mom sits me down at the kitchen table to explain. She takes a deep breath. "When Joan was your age she had a dog she loved."

"Then why doesn't she—"

"And her father ran over it with their car and killed it."

"Asciugamano," I whisper.

"I know," Mom says.

"But it was an accident," I say.

"Well . . ."

"It wasn't an accident?"

"Maybe—her father drank. A lot. And he was probably drunk when he did it."

"Wow. Well, that explains the whiskey bottles she carries around."

"Excuse me?"

"When I meditate, Joan has a sack of whiskey bottles on her back."

Mom bites her lip for a moment. "Her burden," she whispers.

I nod. "I'm really sorry about her dog. And her dad."

"Me too," Mom says and gives me a hug.

I go out to my tree room. I understand why Joan is upset at the thought of a dog, but I bet she'd really love Sirius. And I bet it'd be good for her. Plus, I'd have a friend.

Pookie isn't around because she's always babysitting to make money to buy me a new telescope. No one even told her she had to. But she says she's only babysitting kids who aren't sick, and preferably kids who aren't like her brother, but then she went *Ha-ha!* so I know she's kidding and things are back to normal, only better.

FART!

POOKIE AND COMETS

We're friends again. Just like that! Sometimes the problems are actually the answers. They're loud and scream-y because they're trying to tell you what to do. You just have to listen and figure out what they're saying.

Turns out, Pookie really was the Oort Cloud, hurling rocks at me like comets. It's almost like she found my comet for me. It's not the same as a real comet. I know that. I'm not stupid. But I used to think I had to have my name on a comet so I could live forever. I'm not so sure I need that anymore.

I'm updating my chart of Messier Objects. I'm at the constellation Leo now. It'll be nice having a telescope again. And it'll be nice having Mr. X again, for real. Pookie and I are friends now, but once school starts I'll hardly see her, especially since she's going to join the drama club and she'll be at rehearsals all the time.

That's when I hear the barking.

Coming out of the Subaru that just drove up.

Joan's Subaru.

I run down to greet her.

"You got a dog?" Mom and I say at the same time.

Joan gets out of her car and shrugs. "I don't know what came over me. I went to say no and then . . . I couldn't."

I open the back door and a full-grown black Lab jumps out, practically knocking me down, and kisses me all over.

It's hard to talk when a dog is kissing you all over your face, but I still manage to say, "He's perfect, Joan! How did you know?"

"Your friend told me."

"Mr. X?"

She nods.

"You talked to him?"

"No. It was a Vulcan mind meld."

"Really?"

She shakes her head and laughs. "Of course I talked to him, kiddo."

She roughs up my hair and I give her and Sirius a hug at the same time. "Are you OK with him now? Mr. X, I mean?"

"Sure," she says with a wink. "We Merchant Marines have to stick together."

Sirius kisses me again and I look at his face and here's what I see, other than drool and tiny tufts of hair that stick up from the tops of his ears, which is pretty adorable. His eyes look like the cosmos. No, really. They look like the beginning of that Neil deGrasse Tyson show, *Cosmos: A Spacetime Odyssey*, where you think you're looking at the universe but really it's an eyeball.

Magic.

We throw the toys Joan bought for Sirius, and when a tennis ball ends up in the lake he runs right in without a second thought. Like it's air. Or nothing. I can't believe it.

Joan shrugs. "My dog used to do that."

And then Sirius starts swimming in circles barking and, I swear, smiling! And he won't get out!

"He really loves the water!" Mom says.

Joan's mouth drops open. "That's what my dog did, too."

I squeeze her hand. "It's magic."

She nods slowly. "I think so."

"Did you guys tell Pookie?"

They look at each other and shake their heads.

When Pookie gets back from babysitting, Sirius finally gets out of the water. He shakes himself off on Mom and Joan and me, then pads over to Pookie and sits down in front of her.

"A dog?"

Sirius licks her hand and she pulls it away.

"We got a dog?"

Sirius licks her other hand.

"Hey!"

He dashes to the front porch and comes back with her goggles in his mouth.

"OK, that's weird," Pookie says. "He's winking at me."

"Really?" Joan says. "My dog used to do that! He wants you to go swimming with him!"

Pookie looks at Joan. "Wait. You're OK with a dog? Even after . . . you know, when you were a kid?"

Joan shrugs. "It feels like Leo has come back again."

"Leo?" I say. "Leo? M_{65} and M_{66}! I was just writing that in my chart."

They all look at me.

"It's a sign," I say. "And also, his name is going to be Sirius Leo."

"Works for me," Joan says.

"Pookie," Mom says, "are you going to be OK with this?"

Sirius Leo winks at her again. "Well, I'm not sneezing. Maybe I outgrew my allergies." He drops her goggles on her feet. She rolls her eyes. "I guess we're going swimming now." She says it like she's annoyed, but she's smiling. So are the rest of us.

36

STAR PARTY

I'm hugging Mr. X by the dock as we watch Sirius swim in circles.

Mr. X grunts. "I just have one question for you."

I nod my head into his stomach. I can't explain how I knew he was having a heart attack except . . . "It's the magic of the universe."

"*That's* how you knew I pinch my nose?"

"What?" I back up from him so I can see his face. "Oh, that's obvious. With all the hair in there, how could you not?"

He makes his rumbly sound, but only softly and not in a mad way. "The other part," he says, "I know is magic."

I hug him tighter and this time he actually hugs me back.

"I heard you saying, *You have to live*," I tell him. "That's what kept me alive in the lake."

"I heard *you*," Mr. X says. "That's what kept *me* alive when I was having a heart attack."

I shake my head. "You said it first."

"I don't know which one of us said it first, but the important thing is it worked."

I smile. "It's the magic of the universe."

"Now I believe you, kid."

"You're a uni-sensor, too."

"Julia would roll over in her . . . star. I could never sense anything—when she got new clothes or re-covered the sofas or dropped big hints about her birthday."

"She believes it now."

"I think she does." He looks out over the lake and smiles.

It wasn't the view of the lake Mr. X missed. It was Julia. Family is what he was missing. And now he found us. We can all be family even if we're from different sperm banks.

Sirius dashes out of the water and over to where Pookie is standing in the driveway, looking out to the road.

"Something's up," Mr. X says. "Dogs always know."

I'm uni-sensing something important, too. "Why don't you go help Mom and Joan with the burgers and I'll go check it out."

I walk over to Pookie. In my new board shorts Mom bought me. I know! *Board* shorts. Who would've thought? And they're blue like the sky. And maybe even the water. Pookie got some, too, but hers are black. We also have matching T-shirts from Joan that say THE GOOD THING ABOUT SCIENCE IS THAT IT'S TRUE WHETHER OR NOT YOU BELIEVE IN IT. I'm not sure Joan really believes everything that happened, but at least she's being a good sport about it.

Sirius leans up against me when I reach them. "Who are you waiting for, Pookie?"

"You'll see." Sirius licks Pookie's hand, and instead of saying, "Ew!" she scratches him behind his ears. "I hope they come," she says softly, but I hear her.

"Who?"

But Pookie runs to the end of the driveway because a Jeep is coming down the road. She waves her arms and the Jeep pulls in. Two ladies step out and both of them hug Pookie and she doesn't even seem to mind hugging them back even though they are complete strangers.

Sirius is barking and we're both standing right behind Pookie now and one of the ladies, who reminds me of someone, is staring at me.

"I'm Trieste Sciacchitano," she says.

"Whoa, Mr. X's . . ."

"Sister," she says.

"Wow."

"And this is Beth, my wife."

"Cool!" I say. "This is a real party! Does he know you're coming?"

"We haven't seen each other in over fifty years."

"What!"

Pookie pushes them both toward Mr. X's house, just like she did with me before we knew him, and Trieste and Beth seem just as reluctant.

"It's OK," I say, "he's grump-ish but underneath he's friendly."

"Hasn't changed a bit, then," Trieste says.

As Sirius leads them over to the others, Pookie explains to me that Mr. X had a problem with his sister being gay and that's why Joan didn't care for him.

I shake my head. "I don't think he's like that anymore."

"I don't think he is, either, but his sister needs to see that."

I stare at her and say, inside my head, *Sometimes sisters need help seeing things.*

Pookie rolls her eyes but she's smiling. "I know."

We kind of hold our breath while we watch the awkward handshakes and then Joan says something and everyone laughs, and they all hug and start talking at once.

"Whew," I say.

"No kidding."

"How did you find her?"

"Mom and Joan gave me Internet again because I'm doing something"—she raises her eyebrows—"*positive* with it—making the B&B website and reservation system. So I looked for her on Facebook. It took all of two minutes."

"Wow."

"I know. So much for privacy."

"I'm glad you found her, though. Are you . . . going to look for your dad?"

She shrugs. "Maybe. It's not like I'm desperate or anything."

I feel this big sigh of relief and happiness inside. I think it's my heart smiling. "You want to look through my brand-new telescope that you bought me?"

She musses up my hair and smiles. "Sure, squirt."

We walk down to the dock where we put my telescope tonight because we're actually using the fire pit for a fire. It's awesome. The darker it gets, the brighter the flames are.

Sirius joins us but runs off the end of the dock and splashes into the water for another swim. Mr. X says I'm going to be doing that soon. Ha!

For the first time ever Pookie actually looks through my telescope and how I know is this: She's amazed at what she sees.

I don't even get mad when she says, "Why didn't you ever tell me about this?"

I just say, *Asciugamano!* inside my head and tell her about the Messier Objects.

FART!

MESSIER OBJECTS

Life is pretty messy but it's pretty magical, too. We spend so much time looking past the messier objects to find something better that we don't appreciate how amazing the messier ones are. Sometimes the messier objects are the ones you needed all along, you just didn't see it.

"So," Pookie says softly, "where's Cassiopeia?"

I point the telescope there and she stares through it for a long time.

The grown-ups finally get curious and come over, too, and take turns looking at the Orion Nebula and other cosmic phenomena.

"Wow," Trieste says, "I'm learning so much!"

"Me too," says Mr. X, even though he's looking at his sister and not through the telescope.

"At dawn we can see the Dog Star," I tell everyone.

"At dawn I'll be asleep," Pookie says.

"I'll be up," Mom says. "I love the Dog Star."

And when she says that, Sirius barks from the water.

"Magic," Joan says.

Eventually, everyone drifts over to the campfire to make s'mores except Mr. X and me.

I'm looking up at the Wild Duck Cluster where my grandfather is and I uni-sense him wanting me to look over at Mr. X, which I do and guess what? Mr. X is looking up at the stars, too. I grin and he whips his head around to stare at me and grumble.

"Did you have a nice chat with Julia?" I ask him.

"Go eat your s'mores," he growls, but his face is a little pink and his lips are almost smiling.

I'm still smirking at him and his mouth smiles all the way. He pinches his nose to try to cover it up, but I can see the smile he's hiding.

"Just don't burn the marshmallows," he says with a wink.

For a second I wonder if he's my grandfather and he's come back because nobody really leaves. And then I realize it doesn't matter because he's here now, I'm here now, and we're friends—actually, we're family.

Looking over at the others in front of the fire, I see them laughing. Pookie notices me and holds up a s'more, waving it. I grin back, call Sirius, and run to Mr. X. I grab his hand and we go join our family around the fire that's glowing like the Orion Nebula, throwing out sparks into the night like brand-new stars.

MORE FARTS FROM JULIAN

FART!

EYE MAGIC

Sometimes when I'm looking at something I wonder if everyone sees it the same way, or if *anyone* sees it the same way as me. And how would we know since we can't trade eyeballs?

Did you know that some people can't see color at all? It's true. They can only see in black and white, which is called *achromatopsia* (ay-krome-uh-TOP-see-uh). Some of them live on a tiny island in the Pacific Ocean called Pingelap (PING-ga-lap, which is fun to say), and they're OK with having achromatopsia. I guess if you've only ever seen in black and white, you don't know what color is, so you don't know what you're missing.

It's like when you watch a black-and-white movie that's so good you think it was in color but really it was just your imagination that turned it into color.

Maybe that's how people with achromatopsia see their world. Like magic.

FART!

KITCHEN SCIENCE

Making slime, and rock candy, and eruptions with baking soda and vinegar is awesome. Putting marsh-mallows or Peeps* in the microwave and watching them explode is the best, even if your mom makes you clean the microwave afterward.

*If they're your sister's peeps you should ask first. (She'll say no, which is why I didn't.)

FART!

NOT-SWEAR WORDS

Everyone gets frustrated, and sometimes people feel like swearing, which will only get them in trouble. The trick is to find a not-swear word instead and (bonus!) increase your vocabulary. There are millions of possibilities. When I get tired of *asciugamano*, maybe I'll use the Arabic word for towel instead, *munshifa*, which sounds like min-SHE-fah. That feels pretty good to say.

You can even use proper nouns, like *Kinshasa*. That's the capital of the Democratic Republic of the Congo. Here are some more awesome capitals that are fun to say. If a grown-up glares at you and says, "What did you just say?" you can tell them the name of the capital's country to impress them, and also not get in trouble.

San Salvador! San-SAL-vuh-door! (El Salvador)

Helsinki! Hel-SINK-ee! (Finland)

Jakarta! Juh-KAR-tuh! (Indonesia)

Bratislava! Brah-tis-LAH-vah (Slovakia)

Lusaka! Loo-SAH-kah (Zambia)

If you know someone who gets in trouble for swearing, you can share this idea with them. I should probably share it with Joan.

FART!

LEBRON JAMES AND SIR ISAAC NEWTON

Newton was this British physicist who came up with three laws of motion to explain things like basketball, even though he didn't know about basketball yet because it hadn't been invented. His laws still apply. (Everybody knows who LeBron James is, and if you don't, you can probably guess from context clues.*)

Newton's first law of motion: A ball in motion stays in motion unless something slows it down or stops it.

For example, when LeBron throws the ball, air resistance and gravity slow it down, or another player catches it.

Newton's second law of motion: The heavier a ball is, the more power it takes to give it speed.

LeBron works out so he has a lot of power to throw the ball fast.

Newton's third law of motion: For every action there's an equal and opposite reaction.

When LeBron throws the ball, the ball is actually pushing back against him. He also has to deal with air resistance and gravity except none of it seems to bother him much. In fact, I bet whenever he zips that ball through the air for another three-pointer he's thinking, "Ha! Take that, Mr. Newton!"

*Basketball!

FART!

ORION AND THE PYRAMIDS

Some people think that the three main pyramids at Giza were built to mirror the size and crookedness of the stars in Orion's belt. It makes sense because Orion was important to the ancient Egyptians. So was the Dog Star. If an ancient civilization knew how important Sirius was, they had to be pretty smart.

People have been looking at Orion and Sirius for thousands of years, and thousands of years from now they'll still be looking at them, and calling us an "ancient civilization." Maybe by then we'll know exactly how to get up to the Dog Star.

FART!

GREAT PACIFIC GARBAGE PATCH

The Great Pacific Garbage Patch is a bunch of trash in the Pacific Ocean, like plastic, and "Great" does not mean awesome, but huge. There are garbage patches in the Atlantic and Indian oceans, too. Fish and sea turtles eat the plastic instead of real food, and birds feed it to their chicks who then die.

Pookie says that if I want to worry about something, I should worry about all the trash in the ocean. It's not that I *want* to worry, it's just that I can't help it. And I'm already worried about it. I wish I could help, like those scientists who are breaking down plastics with bacteria. Actually, there's one thing I know I can do. NO plastic water or soda bottles. Or at least recycle them. A Labrador retriever in Wales collected over 26,000 plastic bottles for recycling. If a dog can do it, we can, too.

FART!

DOGS ARE MAGIC

Labrador retrievers make perfect companion and service dogs because they're sweet, gentle, and loyal. And smart. They can even call 911. No, really. They can learn how to press a special button on the phone when there's an emergency. They can also help people with diseases, like diabetes, because they smell chemical changes in the body. And they can sniff out cancer before anyone knows it's there. See? Magic!

ACKNOWLEDGMENTS

With supernova-sized thanks to my incredible agent, Linda Pratt, and the magical team at Scholastic, especially my editor, Andrea Pinkney. Also, thanks to the many people who helped with technical issues in this book, those who have helped me as a writer generally, and everyone who has supported me in my dreams. Bill, you are my guiding star, always.

ABOUT THE AUTHOR

Kathryn Erskine has always loved stargazing and wondering about parallel universes. As a nine-year-old she wandered out to explore the night sky and, when found, quickly learned that her fascination for stargazing was not appreciated. But she kept watching, through her bedroom window, and the back of the car, and outside *with* a grown-up. She also likes Italian, tree houses, and s'mores, and always wears a life jacket (only on boats). She still believes in the magic of the universe.